MR. TROUBLE

NANA MALONE

Mr. Trouble
Copyright 2017 by Nana Malone

This is a work of fiction. Names, characters, places, and incidents either are the product of the author's imagination or are used fictitiously, and any resemblance to actual persons living or dead, business establishments, events, or locales, is entirely coincidental.

Mr. Trouble

COPYRIGHT © 2017 by Nana Malone

All rights reserved. No part of this book may be used or reproduced in any manner whatsoever without written permission of the author except in the case of brief quotations embodied in critical articles or reviews.

Cover Art by Jena brignola

Edited by Daisy Cakes Editing

Proof Editing by Keyanna Butler

Published in the United States of America

1
JARRED

Jarred Maloney cracked open one eye, immediately shutting it as the shaft of sun blazed through to his pounding head. His mouth felt like it was filled with cotton, his tongue sticking to the roof of his mouth something horrid. What the hell happened?

"I see you are awake now."

He cracked open his eyes again, focusing it on the sound of the voice. A very angry voice. It sounded suspiciously like Turner. His best friend did a great angry and broody. Had he passed out at his flat again? Sure enough, Turner was seated in the corner of the room, looking crisp and clean like he always did. Turner was a lawyer and a damn good one, but on occasion he was known to break loose. Jarred had the pictures to prove it. "Hey, Turn," he said, wincing as his voice grated on his own headache.

"Jesus Jarred," Turner said, his words coming out in a heartfelt sigh. "What happened last night?"

Jarred opened his eyes all of the way then, realizing that he wasn't at Turner's flat at all, but a hotel room instead. Well, he thought it was a hotel room. "Will you pull the curtains?" he asked, hoping his voice sounded pleading and pitiful.

Turner chuckled and pointed at the window where the damn light was coming from. "Well if the curtains were still attached to the wall, I could."

Holding up his hand to block the sunlight, Jarred saw that the curtains were dangling from the curtain rod that looked like it was barely attached to the wall itself. Fuck him. How the hell had that happened?

"I assume you had a good time last night," Turner was saying as Jarred rubbed a hand over his face, which still felt numb from the alcohol. "I couldn't understand a word you were saying on your messages."

"I left you messages?"

Turner nodded. "Ten to be exact. Thank God I am smart enough to put the thing on silent or we would be having this discussion hours ago."

"What did I say?"

He shrugged. "Something about crazy women and inviting me to join, what did you call it? Your love den.

Bloody hell Jarred, do you not know what you did last night?"

Amused, Jarred went to push himself up in the bed, his hand colliding with something warm. Make that soft and warm. He frowned.

"Oh yeah, you aren't alone either," Turner offered helpfully.

Jarred grinned and looked over, seeing two women snuggled up to each other. A blonde and a brunette, two of his favorites. Well, all women were his favorites. Tall, short, slim, athletic, curvy. Too bad he couldn't remember a damn thing that happened last night. "I take it from your pinched face you didn't join?" Jarred asked, looking over at Turner.

Turner arched a brow, looking nothing like the bloke who had drunkenly climbed the London Bridge in the middle of the night and pissed off the side to prove that he could. Jarred had the pictures to prove that as well. But, that was before Uni, when Turner got all serious. Jarred had never understood Turner's change. After all, life was about living, right? "I'll pass," he finally said, looking down at his watch. "You're going to be late for your appointment."

"Isn't my appointment with you?" Jarred grumbled, taking one long look at the women beside him. Was his mate really going to make him abandon this bed for him?

"You're still late."

Fuck. Apparently so. With a sigh, Jarred pulled back the covers and stood, the room spinning around him violently. Bile rose up in his throat and he forced it back down. Jarred wasn't going to throw up in front of Turner, again. If he did, he would never hear the end of it. Not like Jarred was going to hear the end of this.

Naked, he looked around the room to get his mind off of the elephants doing salsa in his head and the tornado that had taken up residence in his gut. That was a hole in the wall, looking suspiciously like someone had been pushed hard against it. A flash of memory intruded on the dancing elephants. Him, with the brunette wrapped around his waist, shagging her hard, up against the wall.

Bottles littered the floor, various kinds of liquor and beer that he enjoyed from time to time. Clothes were strewn all over the floor and Jarred bent down to pick up his pants. He felt like shit and Turner was dragging his ass out of the bed. What sense did that make? More importantly, why was he allowing Turner to boss him around?

Oh yeah, he was the one that made sure Jarred got his trust fund checks monthly to keep this lifestyle up.

"Are you just going to stand there with your knob out all day or are you actually going to get dressed?"

Jarred shot him a wry smile as he thrust his legs in his jeans, buttoning them before hunting for his shirt. "What's so important that we need to talk about anyway?"

Turner pushed himself out of the chair and smoothed out his dress pants, shaking out any wrinkles that might have occurred before grabbing his suit coat. "I already told you; I want to discuss it at the office."

Jarred shook his head, the alcohol that he imbibed the night before sloshing around in his stomach uncomfortably. When Turner had called him the other day and said he had something important to discuss, Jarred had wondered why he wouldn't just tell him then. He still didn't understand why Turner was being so secretive about this entire conversation, but it was obvious he wasn't going to breathe a word of it until they were sitting downtown.

One of the women in the bed stirred and Jarred looked back, taking in the creamy expanse of her back in the process. Turner was being an ass this morning making him leave like this. There were still hours of fun in that bed and Turner was being stupid to not want some of that action. With reluctance, Jarred got dressed and Turner walked him downstairs, allowing him to stop off to grab a cup of coffee in the process to counter the effects of the alcohol. When they walked outside, a chill hung in the air, tearing through the thin material of Jarred's dress shirt. The weather was starting to turn now, the days growing shorter and the temperature a far cry from the warmth of the summer. Jarred glanced around, recognizing some of the landmarks, though he still didn't know how he had ended up over here in East London. A few blocks to the left was the O2 Arena. The hotel was one on the fringes of the city, one that wasn't particularly frequented by the wealthy of London. But it was near some of the clubs he enjoyed, which only made sense that he would go there instead of his own flat. One of his rules since Susan left, was never take anyone back to his flat.

"Aw man," Jarred said as they approached Turner's car. "You couldn't drive the Porsche at least?"

Turner looked at him over the roof of his four door sedan, a frown on his face. "You know I don't drive that car."

"Yeah, yeah," Jarred grumbled, grabbing the passenger side door handle and yanking it open. "Just because your father gave it to you doesn't mean you don't have to drive it. I mean, this is a chick car and not in a good way." Turner's father was a real estate mogul who had built a veritable empire in Europe. Turner was his only son and for the love of Christ, Jarred couldn't understand why Turner hated the fact that his father was filthy rich.

The two of them had met as boys in school, both the products of wealthy men who expected their sons to follow in their footsteps. They'd had many a scrape and narrow escape throughout the years and though Jarred gave Turner a hard time, he loved his mate. As far as he was concerned, they were family.

"Just shut up and get in," Turner said as he climbed in the driver's seat. Jarred climbed in the car and they were off, heading toward downtown where Turner's office was located. Jarred leaned back on the seat and sipped his coffee, his head pounding behind his eyeballs. He enjoyed a good time and apparently had one of the best last night, even if he couldn't remember it. *Is it still a good time if you're trying to numb out the pain?* He shoved that thought aside.

"You can't keep doing this, J," Turner said after a few moments, his voice breaking the silence in the car. "You have to straighten yourself out. Go to work. Find a hobby. Something."

Jarred grinned. "I have one."

"Getting arse faced on a nightly basis is not a hobby."

"It could be," Jarred retorted, draining the rest of his coffee before placing the cup in the holder on the console. Hell, he'd made it a hobby over the last few years. He was known in the social scene, never turned away from a party and though his father hated the fact that his son was a loser in his eyes, at least his son hadn't landed in jail yet.

"Come on Jarred," Turner said as he pulled his car into the parking garage connected to the office building. "Surely there's something you want to do with your life."

"Oh, you mean like you?" Jarred asked with a harsh laugh. Turner had sold out for the working man's life, a life Jarred couldn't understand. "Forgive me if I don't want to work my ass off for the middle man."

"Sod off," Turner muttered as he parked the car. "I keep your ass out of a sling. Remember that."

Jarred grinned and climbed out of the car, following Turner into the lift that would lead them to Turner's firm office. "And I pay you very well to do so."

Turner let out a bark of laughter. "You pay me nothing. Your father pays my legal bills."

Jarred shrugged. "Same thing." After all, it was all to be his once the old man kicked the bucket. What he was going to do with it when that time came, he didn't know.

The lift doors opened and a long legged blonde entered the lift, giving them both a once over before she turned around. Jarred took in her toned body encased in a suit appreciatively before looking over at Turner, nodding toward her. Turner's head nearly fell off of his shoulders as he shook it vehemently, his eyes warning Jarred not to do what he already knew was coming. It was time for a bit of fun this morning. Jarred gave Turner a quick grin and tapped her on her shoulder, a cloud of expensive perfume filling his nostrils as she turned around. "Yes?" she asked, an amused smile on her face.

"I'm sorry to bother you," Jarred started out, "but my friend here, he needs to get laid and quick."

Her eyes widened as she looked over at Turner, who looked like he wanted to be anywhere but here for the moment. "Is that right?"

"Desperate," Jarred added, giving her a knowing look and nearly unable to contain his laughter. "You would be doing him a favor."

"He's not, don't listen to him," Turner finally forced out, coming out in a choked laugh. "He's mentally unstable."

"Unstable," Jarred said. "But still able to get laid."

The doors opened and she bailed out, her heels clicking hard on the polished wood floor as she hurried away. Jarred waited until the doors closed again before he burst into laughter, Turner socking him hard on the shoulder with his fist. "Please don't try to do me any favors. Bloody hell, she will never speak to me again."

"I think she was thinking about it until you threw out the whole mental instability piece," Jarred answered, shoving his hands in his pockets. "You do need to get laid Turner. That necktie has gotten too tight around your neck."

"Bugger off," he said as the doors opened again and he walked out, his fists balled at his sides.

"Payback's a bitch," Jarred reminded him as he followed his friend, winking at the receptionist as they entered Turner's domain. "Come on Turner, I'm only trying to help."

"Sit down, Jarred."

Jarred sat down in one of the comfortable leather chairs in front of Turner's large oak desk, resisting the urge to prop his feet up on it. He'd already pushed his friend enough and it wasn't even ten in the morning. "What's up? What's so important?"

Turner rested his elbows on the desk, his expression suddenly serious. "It's about your trust fund Jarred."

Jarred groaned. "Don't tell me that he wants to cut it back again. He's already tried that route." His father had attempted to cut the money in half a few months ago in an effort to rile him up and it had worked, just not in the way that he wanted it to happen. Instead, Jarred had racked up tabs all over London in his father's name and as a result, Harrison Maloney had been driven so crazy by the amount of collectors wanting their money that he'd restored the amount without a word. Jarred had proven a point to him that day, one that he thought his father wouldn't forget anytime soon.

"He's cutting you off totally."

Jarred's grin slid from his face. "What did you say?"

Turner sighed, looking weary all of a sudden. "I'm sorry Jarred. He's cutting the money at the end of the month. I've been instructed to drop the account effective immediately."

Jarred rose from his chair, pushing it hard until it toppled over on the floor with a loud thud. The sound sliced through his pounding head but he didn't care. "Cut me off?" Jarred was his son, his sole heir. "He can't do that."

"He already has," Turner replied softly.

Jarred looked at him, panic and rage flowing in his blood. No way in hell he was going to let his father do this.

2

KINSLEY

"No, no, no."

Kinsley grabbed the letter off of her flat entrance door, her earlier good mood of her hellacious day ending now souring once more. *"Ms. Wells,"* it stated, the words on a neatly typed letterhead depicting the name of the building's owners. *"We are in the process of selling our flats and will disband the lease agreements at the end of the month. As a current occupant of one of our flats, we are giving you the first opportunity to purchase this one before it is listed. The current value of the flat is £450,000. The initial installment of £100,000 will be due at the end of the month to secure the impending purchase. As we start to prepare our flats for purchase, a building wide fumigation will take place at the end of the week. Please make other arrangements for two to three days. You will not be allowed back into the flat during this time. Please contact our real estate office with payment options and further details."*

She reread the letter again, panic welling in her throat. 450,000 pounds? That was an obscene amount of money for someone in her position. Tears clouded her eyes but she blinked them away, wrangling with the door to get it unlocked and walking inside the cool interior. She could not lose it right now, not where everyone could see at least.

After placing the groceries on the counter, she picked up the letter once more, hoping that she had been wrong in her first two reads. *Nope.* Everything was still there. Not only did she have to come up with 100,000 pounds in three weeks, she also had to vacate the place for a few days while they sprayed for bugs. Great. This was just great. She threw the letter on the counter and leaned against it, looking at the space she had leased for three years now. It was the perfect size for her, with one bedroom that overlooked a small walled garden and was close to the tube station, allowing her a quick way in and out to work each day. The neighborhood was quaint and quiet, where everyone waved to her as she walked down the street. She loved the flat and did not want to move. But it was so much more than just a flat. It showed her what she'd been able to do, without anyone's help. She'd done this. All on her own. She'd built her world and now it was crumbling.

Slamming a fist on the counter, Kinsley let the tears fall. Now what was she supposed to do? The place was rent controlled. There was no way she could afford to move to a similar place. She paid her rent on time, never complained to the landlord and kept the place in great condition. *But that's not enough is it? Working hard will never be good enough.*

Fishing her cell out of her purse, she quickly found her best friend Rachel's number and pressed the button, listening to it dial her number in her ear. "Hello?" she said a minute later.

"Rachel," Kinsley choked out.

"Kinsley? What's wrong?" She and Rachel had been friends since they were little, considering they were also cousins, but she was more like a sister to Kinsley than just a cousin. Many a time Kinsley had wondered what she would do without her in her life. "They're selling my flat."

"What?" Rachel's voice was calm, even. "What do you mean?"

Kinsley sighed, tears gathering in her eyes once more. "The flat. The owners are selling them. I have to come up with 100,000 quid by the end of the month or I'm out."

"100,000 pounds? Are you serious?"

"Unfortunately," she muttered. "They are fumigating too. I have to find somewhere else to stay at the end of the week."

"That sucks," Rachel replied, disdain in her voice. "I can't believe they would do that. But if you need, you can always come stay with me."

"Thank you, I love you, but the commute from North London will kill me. I know I can probably provision a company flat for the time being," Kinsley said, wiping the tear that had escaped down her cheek unchecked. "But what am I going to do?" She had nowhere else to go. Her job as an administrative assistant paid decently but nowhere near enough to front that kind of money. Besides, Kinsley's tuition to continue the last semester of her Master's degree was due and she was so, so close to having it complete. An advanced degree meant new open doors at her job and she couldn't afford to take a step back. Not when she'd worked so hard.

"Times like this I wished I lived closer, and that Jamison's family wasn't here to stay," Rachel continued. "I'm sorry Kinsley."

Kinsley heard the worry in her cousin's voice and knew that if she could, Rachel would do anything to help, including letting her stay with her and her fiancé, Jamison. They were currently on the countdown to their wedding day and with Jamison being from Ireland, his family had come to London to stay the rest of the time to help out with the wedding plans. "It's okay Rach," she finally said, drawing in a deep breath. "I'll figure out something."

"Maybe you can find another job," she suggested. "You know, to supplement the extra money?"

Kinsley snorted. "It would have to be the best paying job in the world." Flipping burgers wasn't going to work in a pinch.

"Okay, well maybe you should just talk to them you know? You're a good tenant. They will want to keep you around."

Kinsley shook her head. While she was a good tenant, she was also the difference between a paltry sum and a payday on an older flat. There was no way they were going to give her an inch. Kinsley was going to be kicked out of the home she had made unless she hit the lotto or had a rich family member that was about to kick the bucket.

"Don't give up so soon," Rachel said. "You have access to the company flats right? Go stay there."

"That's really my only option." Kinsley thought about the nice flat in the wealthy side of town that was owned by her boss, Maloney Motors. Maloney Motors was one of the biggest automotive companies in Europe, specializing in luxury cars. They even had an F1 team. She worked for the owner of the company, Harrison Maloney, in the company headquarters based here in London as his administrative assistant.

Part of her job was to keep track of the visitors all over the world and stick them in some of the flats that the company owned for their comfort so naturally she had the keys to all of them. There was one that wasn't being utilized currently and wouldn't be for a few weeks at least. Technically, she could move in there temporarily to escape the fumigation. "I don't know, though," Kinsley said, biting her lip. "What if I'm caught? I mean, I've always been told to take what I need, but this seems like overstepping."

"Oh come on, like old Maloney would can you," Rachel laughed. "Do it and ask for forgiveness later."

She looked around her own flat, knowing full well she couldn't afford to rent out a room for the weekend on her current money, especially if she was going to try and finagle a way to pay for this place. "I'm tired. I'm going to go."

"Wait," Rachel barked into the phone. "Don't forget about your fitting tomorrow for your bridesmaid dress. I can't believe we are getting down to the weeks now. I am so excited but I'm worried I won't fit into my dress with all of this food Jamison's mom is fixing."

"You'll be fine," Kinsley answered, a soft smile on her face. Rachel was going to be the perfect bride and even if she gained two stone, Jamison was still going to love her. They were disgustingly in love with each other and every time Kinsley was around the two of them, it made her question why she hadn't found anyone yet. "I'll be there."

"You better be," she said before clicking off. Kinsley placed the phone on the counter, her eyes sliding to the infernal letter that had effectively ruined her day. What was she going to do? Kinsley was the last of the Wells line, her parents dying in a car accident when she was fifteen. The roads had been slick with rain and they had been coming back from a weekend in the country. The police had stated they hadn't even seen the tree in the middle of the road. She had been moved to her aunt and uncle's home and she and Rachel had become roommates. After graduation, she had gone to arts college and Kinsley had found the job with the Maloney corporation, able to save up enough to move out and move on with her life. But now, she felt like she was taking steps backward in her life. She was on the verge of acquiring her MBA, which would make her eligible for a manager's position that had opened recently, but until she got that piece of paper in her hands, there wasn't a thing she could do. Kinsley was stuck.

"What have I done to deserve this?" she asked aloud, looking up at the tiled ceiling. It was like fate was messing with her and she didn't know what to do about it.

3

JARRED

Jarred was forced to wait until the next morning to confront his father about his trust fund. Though he would have preferred to confront him right after Turner had dropped the bomb, his father was out of town and Jarred wanted to talk to him face-to-face.

He walked to the Maloney headquarters in the heart of the city, the cool air clearing his head and allowing him some time to think about how he was going to approach the old man and tell him his plan was stupid. What was he trying to do to him? Break him? Make Jarred into the man that he was? It wasn't going to work. He wasn't his father. Even the half dozen whiskey shots Jarred had consumed at the nearby pub hadn't calmed his anger or changed the fact that he was never going to be Harrison Maloney. Harrison Maloney was all business. And he was the black sheep. The unwanted one.

Walking into the old brownstone, Jarred punched the lift button and stepped in as soon as the doors opened, hitting the top floor where his father's offices were. While multi-million dollar companies preferred sleeker, modern office buildings, dear old dad preferred old money ways, keeping the same building that Jarred's grandfather had started the family business in long ago. The cars were made in a facility in the industrial section of the city, but the magic, as his father liked to call it, happened here. The company had one of those sleek buildings of course over in Kinston upon Thames where the majority of the employees worked, but this, this was the hub for most of the senior executives.

The lift doors opened and he stepped out, his steps muffled by the plush carpeting. His father's assistant was seated at her desk outside his office, her eyes widening as she saw him approaching. "M-Mr. Maloney," she stammered, standing abruptly. "Your father is about to go on a conference call. If you would like to wait a moment."

Jarred held up his hand, silencing her next words as he stalked past. "I'll only be a moment."

She opened her mouth to object but he didn't wait to hear what she said, pushing open the door and walking in. His father was seated at his desk, his phone in his hand when Jarred entered, his eyebrows raising in surprise. "Jarred."

"Dad," he said tightly. His father's eyes narrowed at the sound of his name and not the customary father, which gave Jarred slight satisfaction that he was pissed off. Good.

Placing the phone back on the receiver, he laced his fingers and stared at his son. "Well? What is it?"

"My trust fund," Jarred forced out, hating the way his father acted like he didn't know what was up. He knew why he was here.

His father leaned over and pressed a number on his phone console. "Kinsley, reschedule my call for ten please."

"Yes sir," she replied before he clicked off, turning his attention back toward his son. Jarred clenched his fists tightly at his side, staring him directly in the eye. "What the hell are you trying to do to me?"

He laughed. "That is a loaded question Jarred. The same could be said of you."

"I'm not you," Jarred bit out.

He shook his head slowly. "That is correct. You are far from the way I was at your age. Do you know I was making multi-million dollar deals at age twenty?"

Jarred hated when his father did that, making him feel like he wasn't worthy enough to be his son. Jarred had tried to be successful like him once and it hadn't worked out.

"Have you heard from Susan lately? You were a fool to lose her."

Jarred gritted his teeth, thinking about his ex-fiancée for the first time in weeks. They'd been broken up for four months, but he was surprised at the burn of bitterness in his throat when he thought of her. He should have completely forgotten her by now. She wasn't anything to him.

Susan's family ran in the same social circles as his family did so it wasn't surprising when they hooked up. Two years later, Jarred had bit the bullet and bought a ring, presenting it to her one night over dinner. It had seemed like the next step. After all, they had been living together. Susan was very involved in the charitable social scene, though Jarred always thought it was because she liked the limelight and not actually helping people.

He'd loved her. He'd actually thought he could do it too. Be that bloke. The kind of son his father was proud of. And he'd put everything into that relationship. Even when everything in his being screamed that it wasn't working, that it didn't fit, he'd forced it. Hell, even Turner had seemed confused that he wanted to marry her. The two of them had never gotten along. But damn it, Jarred had tried.

But it wasn't long after he'd proposed that he'd seen the chinks in her armor. The way nothing he did was ever enough. The way she spent money like it was water. The way she envied her other friends with their even richer husbands. Sure, he was a drunken sod now, but he'd had plans. He wanted to take over his father's F1 team. He had a lot of ideas to make them a major contender. But that hadn't been enough for her. She'd said it was common.

Even for his own fiancée, he hadn't been enough. She'd left in the middle of the night, the sparkling diamond on the empty pillow beside him, with a note that said, "I'm worth more than this. I can do better." Not even a month later, she was attached to someone even richer than his father. Her leaving had been part of his alcoholic binge and another black mark on his record according to his father. "This isn't about her," Jarred said through clenched teeth.

His father smirked. "I saw her the other night. She's looking great, too much of a woman for you apparently."

His family hadn't even asked what had happened. They'd assumed he'd fucked up. That was an admission that burned in his gut. Turner though. He'd known. But he'd also been happy to see her go. "Just give me back my trust fund and I'll get out of your sight."

"It's not that easy," his father said, leaning back in his chair, lacing his hands over his suit clad stomach. "It wasn't just my call, Jarred. The stakeholders in this company, the ones that keep the lights on and production running are concerned with your behavior and the future of this company. To be frank, I was forced to make a decision, son, and it's for your own good."

"By cutting me off?" he asked. "What will they say now when I'm living on the streets and begging for scraps?"

He laughed. "You are far from being a beggar on the streets Jarred. God, you are just like your mother, a consummate actress when she wants to be."

"Sod off," he muttered even as the blood boiled just under the surface.

"Tsk, tsk," he said, shaking his head at his son. "There are conditions to getting your trust money back, Jarred. He left you an out, of course. Every business dealing should have an out. All you have to do is show me that son I know is hiding under that booze fueled outer shell."

He heard his words over the dull roar of his anger. "Outs?"

His father nodded. "Two to be exact. If you take care of both of them, then I'll reinstate your money. Actually, I'll double them and vow to never touch them again. How does that sound? I'll even sign a contract."

"What are they?" he asked, eyeing his father. In his warped mind, they could be anything but he was willing to at least listen and find out. After all, he needed his money back. He was right, though, as much as Jarred hated to admit it. It would be months before he would need to worry, but the trust fund monthly was his cushion, one less thing he needed to worry about until now. *It's also your prison.* Jarred shoved the thought to the back of his mind. He *needed* that money. After all, he was the ne'er do well son.

How could he stay in his role if he actually had to work? *Maybe finally do what you want?* No. Not going to happen.

The old man looked almost gleeful as he leaned forward, resting his elbows on the desk. "First, you must become involved in this company in some capacity. He didn't work his ass off to make a future for you to have you throw it all away. This is our family's legacy Jarred, your legacy, and I expect you to be involved. Hell, even if it's with the stupid Formula One team you love so much. I don't care. But either way, you're going to work."

Jarred sighed inwardly. He hated the idea. He didn't want to do what his father did day in and day out. It was boring, grueling work with very little return if you took the money out of it. His father spent half of his life in this office and he didn't care to do the same. "I can pick?" Jarred asked finally.

He nodded. "Anything you want to get involved in Jarred will be better than what you are doing currently."

"Fine," Jarred said, seeing no other way. There would be something he could get involved in with very little impact on his current life. "What's the other condition?"

The elder Maloney looked at his son with a gleam in his eye. "You have to settle down."

Jarred swallowed. "What exactly does that mean?"

"Find a girl, a decent girl," his father responded. "Someone that you wouldn't mind marrying one day and having a brood of kids. If you can find one that is willing to stick with you. I mean, you had a gem in Susan and you let her slip through your fingers."

Jarred knew he shouldn't want to impress his father, but right now, he could punch the smirk off of his face and not feel one ounce of remorse for doing so. He wanted to show the old man, he wanted to prove to himself that he could be so much more than the man that his father made him out to be. He wasn't this loser, but a man who wanted to live more, see more, experience more than just these four walls and a shitload of work that went with it. More importantly, he didn't want to become this man before him. And he sure as hell wasn't going to be pushed into another relationship. "I already found someone."

His father's eyes widened. "What? When did this happen?"

"A few months ago. We've been keeping it under wraps." Jarred said quickly. Hey, it could have happened. He just couldn't remember any of the women he'd met over the last week to say definitively that he hadn't met the woman of his future. "She's great, exactly what you are talking about."

"Well," his father replied, apparently buying the story, "then I have to meet this paragon of virtue. Bring her over to the house next week for dinner. We will celebrate your relationship."

Jarred's jaw clamped shut. *Great*. If he attempted to get himself out of this, his father would know immediately that he was lying. "Yeah sure, we will be there."

The elder Maloney eyed him for a moment. "Good," he finally said. "Can't wait to meet this woman."

Jarred wanted to say he couldn't either but put on a tight smile. Now he had to find the woman that would agree to this mess. Should be fun times.

4

KINSLEY

Kinsley gathered her purse and walked to the lift, thinking that a greasy basket of fish and chips would be perfect for lunch today. She was tired. She'd tossed and turned last night, worrying about what the hell she was going to do. No matter how she calculated the money left in her checking and savings account, there was no way she could afford the flat or to even consider taking out a loan. The bank would laugh her straight out the door. She was going to have to give up the place.

The lift arrived and Kinsley stepped in, pressing the button for the first floor. Moving was her only choice. What else could she do?

"Wait. Hold the doors."

Kinsley looked up to see Jarred Maloney striding toward her, her finger holding the open button so he could enter as well. "Thanks," he said as the lift doors closed. "How do you work for that bloody bastard anyway?"

"Excuse me?" she asked, eyes wide. He looked over and she was momentarily stunned. She'd only met him a handful of times, but all of London knew who he was. He was flippin' Jarred Maloney, sole heir to Maloney Motors and total playboy. He had the looks to back the claims up, with his dark hair and startling green eyes. The gossip mags called him knicker melting. They weren't kidding. This kind of close proximity had her heart pounding ever so slightly. He had a killer body to go with the killer face. And she knew it because his abs were flashed more than once all over the rags. Gossip magazines were her only vice. She refused to feel guilty about devouring them. It was usually the closest she'd ever come to meeting someone like Jarred.

But as mouthwatering as he was, he was miles away from Kinsley's idea of the perfect bloke. She preferred, well, someone a bit more toned down. Pretty was nice, but pretty would eventually want to upgrade to a supermodel. Steady and dependable worked better.

"That bastard, my father," he grumbled, leaning against the wall of the lift as they descended. "He must pay well."

Kinsley smelled the faint whiff of whiskey and frowned, wondering who in the world drank before lunch. Why had he visited his father this morning? No doubt to ask for more money. Rumor was Jarred Maloney lived off of his father's money and he wasn't afraid to tell anyone that fact. Kinsley couldn't even imagine doing such a thing. She worked hard to be where she was at, even if the world was now against her. Her eyes welled up and she turned away. Oh no, she wasn't going to cry in front of this twat. No matter how hot he was in his current sullen mood. "I'm sorry Mr. Maloney, I don't know what you mean."

He laughed then, the sound sending a shiver down her spine. "Well, well loyal and pretty. My father is quite lucky to have you on his team."

"I just do my job," she swallowed, wondering what was taking the lift so long to get to the bottom floor.

"What's your name?"

She looked over at him, seeing interest in his eyes with an adorable grin on his face. Oh shit. No wonder he was touted as a sex symbol in the media pages. That grin could melt panties the world round. Kinsley tried to ignore the fact that her stomach was doing funny flips and gave him her best frown in return. "It's Kinsley Wells. We've met before. More than once."

"Kinsley," he murmured, making her name sound sexy. "Do you like to have fun Kinsley?"

Heat suffused her face. She wanted to ignore him, pretend that he wasn't even standing next to her, the whiskey no longer as overpowering as the spicy scent of his aftershave.

It smelled faintly of oranges. She loved oranges. "I-I have fun Mr. Maloney."

"Jarred," he said, his grin widening. "You're perfect, Kinsley."

She wasn't sure what he meant but thankfully didn't have to find out, the lift doors opening and startling them both. Kinsley gave him a quick smile and hurried out, her pulse racing. For a brief moment, she had forgotten about her money troubles and basked in Jarred Maloney's attention. Like an idiot. No doubt he would forget her name as soon as he walked out of the lift, but that was fine with her. He'd called her perfect. What had that meant?

Her phone chimed and she fished it out of her purse as she walked outdoors, shivering as the wind cut through her thin coat. "Hello?"

"Kinsley are you on lunch yet?"

"I am," Kinsley said, glad that Rachel had called her. "Care to grab a bite?"

"I can't," Rachel sighed into the phone. "I have so much to do during my break unfortunately." Rachel worked downtown at an arts gallery and absolutely loved her job. It was one of the reasons she had met Jamison. "I was just wondering if you decided on moving into that flat or not."

It was Kinsley's turn to sigh. "I don't have a choice. I just hope it doesn't cost me my job." She couldn't afford to lose her only source of income.

"You'll be fine," Rachel insisted. "I've got to go pick up the programs now. Let's go out for drinks tomorrow night. I need to get out of this house before I go crazy."

She signed off before Kinsley had a chance to tell her about the weird lift conversation with Jarred Maloney. Rachel was hooked on the social media sites and more than once had mentioned the man's name in passing. Jarred Maloney was definitely a hot commodity, so much so that he had his own webpage dedicated to his antics. Kinsley had to admit to herself that she had visited it a time or two, living it up through someone else's photos and experiences. Between work and her degree, she had no room for clubbing and the like. Her idea of a fun time, as Jarred had asked her about, was having a brownie on a Friday night. Besides Rachel, she had no one else in her life socially. Damn, maybe it was time to get some friends.

Kinsley dropped her phone back into her bag and walked the block over to the small pub that she frequented occasionally, knowing she should hold on to the money instead of buying lunch. She could hold her lunch money for the rest of her life and never gather up enough money to pay for her flat. She was doomed to start the search for a new place, no matter how much she didn't want to do it.

5

JARRED

THE NEXT NIGHT, Jarred and Turner sat at a pub not far from Turner's flat, one known to have great karaoke and cold ale. It wasn't Jarred's usual haunt, but Turner liked the place and since he needed for Turner to stay on his side with this whole mess with his father, Jarred had relented. "I can't believe he would do that to you," Turner was saying as he polished off his beer, wiping his mouth with his napkin. "Push you into a relationship? What sense does that make? He doesn't remember how well that went with Susan?"

"No sense at all," Jarred admitted with a shrug. His father wanted complete and utter control of Jarred's life and however that could happen, he was going to push until he broke his son down. "Worse yet, I told him I was already dating someone."

Turner laughed. "Did you happen to mention that to either one of the ladies in the bed the other morning? Perhaps they were unaware you were looking for a relationship."

"Sod off," Jarred muttered, snatching up his pint. He shouldn't have lied to his father, dug himself a bigger hole, but he wanted to wipe the smirk off of his face and that was the only possible way to do that. Now if he didn't find someone to agree to pretend to be his girlfriend before the end of the week, he was going to have to find a job because he could kiss the money goodbye. It was a hard place he'd wedged himself in. "Help me think you tosser."

"You could call Susan, see if she would come back," Turner offered.

"No. And *fuck* no." Jarred shook his head, running a hand through his hair. "Besides, no can do. Heard she was shackled to Baron."

"Baron?" Turner asked, surprise on his face. "Baron Temsfield?"

Jarred nodded, thinking about how he felt when he'd read the headline himself. Susan had wasted no time moving on. Baron was one of their chums from school, his father a business and trade mogul who was wealthier than either Turner's or Jarred's father. Baron had just gone through a nasty divorce with his first wife so it was quite the surprise that he would jump back into the fray so soon.

But whatever. Jarred didn't care about what happened to her.

"Wow," Turner said, sitting back in his chair. "I'm sorry."

"Don't be," Jarred said nonchalantly. He didn't want it to bother him, but it did, knowing that he'd been bowled over for someone wealthier. He had cared about her. It wasn't any kind of deep-hearted, soul bending love by any means, but they had respected each other and the affection was there, or at least he'd thought it was. "She's gone. I've got to find someone to impress my father so I can get my life back."

"What are you going to offer the woman?"

Jarred turned to Turner. "What?"

Turner signaled for another pint. "You know, to go with you on this."

"Besides my good looks?" Jarred joked.

Turner rolled his eyes. "Yes, besides that."

Jarred shrugged. "I don't know. Money probably shouldn't be a thought considering I won't have any if I can't pull this off."

"Money makes the world go round," Turner muttered as his pint appeared. The door opened and they both turned to see two women walk in, chatting with each other as they walked past. Jarred immediately picked out his father's assistant as one of them. She was brunette and petite, with an oval face and wide expressive eyes that had looked at him with disdain just the day before in the lift. While she wasn't the obvious type of beauty he usually went for, there was something about her that had him intrigued. It had to be the eyes. Or maybe the way her full lips moved when she spoke. Or her voice, quiet, but with a hit of steel. Maybe it was because she could put up with his father. The other woman was a striking redhead, her hands moving this way and that as they seated themselves at the bar not far from Jarred and Turner.

"Hey, what about her?" Turner asked, gesturing toward the women.

Jarred took one look at Kinsley and shook his head. "No."

"The redhead? Really? She looks like your type."

The redhead. Why hadn't that been his first thought? She was his type, long legged and animated, no doubt having the ability to win over his father. "Um yeah, she will work."

Turner chuckled. "You sound like a pig being led to slaughter. Why don't you just tell your father to sod off and go get a job like I did? I don't have to depend on my father for anything and have told him that time and time again."

Jarred looked at his friend. "Well, you do have a degree behind your name and have turned into some poor bloke who will never pick up a woman with that shirt you have on."

Turner looked down at the checkered shirt and frowned. "What's wrong with my shirt?"

Jarred chuckled and grabbed his pint, sliding off of the stool. "Wish me luck."

Turner just shook his head as Jarred walked over to the ladies, leaning against the bar beside the redhead. "A drink for these lovely ladies," he said to the bartender. "On me."

The redhead swiveled around and her eyes went round with surprise. "Oh my god, you're Jarred. Jarred Maloney."

"At your service," he grinned. Kinsley peered at him over her friend's head and frowned, but he ignored her. He was looking forward to this conversation. "And you are?"

"Engaged," Kinsley blurted out as the redhead started to speak. "She's getting married in a few weeks."

"Kinsley," the redhead replied, embarrassed as she turned to her friend. Kinsley shrugged and gave him a smirk, satisfied that she got her point across. Her friend turned back to him, a blush on her cheeks. "I'm sorry, I don't know what's wrong with her. I'm Rachel. It's great to meet you."

"I'm hurt that I didn't get to meet you sooner," Jarred said, giving Rachel a wounded look. "You have taken my breath away." He heard a snort coming from behind Rachel and couldn't help but wonder what he'd done to get on Kinsley's bad side.

"Wow, that's so nice of you," Rachel smiled, fluttering her lashes. "Wasn't that nice Kinsley?"

"Sounds like a line to me," Kinsley replied, shooting daggers at him. The drinks arrived and Jarred grabbed his now full pint, holding it up to Rachel. "Well, let's toast to a happy marriage for you then. He's a lucky bloke."

Rachel held up her drink, giving Kinsley a look before she reluctantly did the same, clinking her glass against his. "Good evening ladies," he said, pushing away from the bar and walking back toward Turner, who had an expectant look on his face.

"Well?"

"She's getting married," Jarred replied, his eyes on Kinsley.

"Damn," Turner said, echoing Jarred's sentiments. "What about her friend? Did you ask her?"

Jarred watched as Kinsley conversed with her friend, taking in her prim blouse and slacks that left everything to the imagination. She was snobbish, apparently detested him and was in cahoots with his father. Wait a minute. "She's my father's assistant," he said slowly, a plan forming in his mind. That meant she had already impressed his father and would be the absolute last person he would expect Jarred to bring.

"Oh wow," Turner announced. "That's it, mate. Bloody hell, she's perfect. Your father already approves of her. Imagine the look on his face when you show up with her on your arm."

"Yeah," Jarred murmured absently. Only problem with Little Miss Uptight, he had to get her to agree to this. And with the way she had dressed him down tonight, it was going to be one hell of a mountain to climb. He needed leverage and he needed it quickly. How he was going to do that, he didn't know, but good thing he was resourceful.

6

KINSLEY

Kinsley opened the door to the flat and groaned, dropping her suitcase just inside the foyer. She hated having to sneak into this flat, but she had no other choice. Besides, her housing could be a great deal worse. The flat was in an upscale neighborhood, where she was certain that the flats were far more expensive than the one she was trying to keep. It was posh and the décor reflected the contemporary style. It looked sterile and not at all comfortable, but Kinsley knew she couldn't be picky. It was furnished and more importantly free, two reasons she had decided to go this route.

Picking up her suitcase, Kinsley shut the door and walked into the kitchen, dropping the set of keys in the small dish that sat on the granite counter along with the small bag of food she had picked up on the way. Today she had made her decision. With the fumigation due for the morning, she had blocked off the schedule for the flat and grabbed some things to get her through the next few days before heading over here, hoping that this wasn't going to get her in trouble.

It was a good thing that she controlled the calendar so the flat was officially hers and she planned to not even leave a trace of her visit when she left. The sun had already set as she had her meager supper and cleaned up after herself, moving onto the bedroom which boasted a bed three times the size of her own.

If her nerves weren't so racked about being here, she might enjoy the plush carpeting under her feet or step out onto the balcony that gave an impressive view of the city. But instead she hurried through her toiletry and climbed in between the sheets, reveling in their luxuriousness. What would it be like to live like this constantly, to never worry about money? Jarred Maloney's grin crossed her mind and she sighed, thinking of the way he'd hit on Rachel the night before.

She hated to admit to herself, but she had been jealous. Jealous that he clearly hadn't remembered her from the lift ride, jealous that she wasn't the first one he approached. All of her life she knew that Rachel was prettier than she was, more outgoing, and definitely popular throughout school. Kinsley, while she loved her cousin dearly, couldn't help but wish that Rachel would hurry and marry her love so she would be taken off the market. It was selfish yes, but last night had not been the first time that she had been overlooked for Rachel. It stung knowing she'd never be the first choice.

With a groan, Kinsley punched at the pillow, staring into the darkness. Rachel being picked up by hot men was the least of her worries. She was about to lose her home and had no idea what she was going to do. The other flats in that area for rent were beyond her price range and the only place she could find that would give her a bit of money at the end of the month was a thirty-minute commute at least.

She hadn't ever owned a car so that was out of the question. She had one other option, one that she hated to even consider. She could move back home with her aunt and uncle. Their home was close to a tube and likely would be rent free. The thought, though, made her nauseous. Go back under someone else's roof? When her parents had died, they'd taken her in. Done their duty. But they'd never been warm. No way was she going back. Especially not as a failure. she'd rather sleep on the street. She supposed she could get a flat-mate, but one bad experience in Uni had soured her on the idea.

A thud jolted her out of her thoughts, making the pictures on the wall rattle as it happened again. "What on earth?" she asked herself, grabbing her wrap and climbing out of the bed. It sounded as if someone was trying to burst through the wall. Hurrying down the hall, Kinsley made quick work of the locks against her better judgement and opened the door as the noise sounded again. "Oh no."

Jarred was sitting in the hallway, his back against the door next to Kinsley's, a half empty bottle of liquor still clenched tightly in his grasp. The stench of whiskey permeated the air and Kinsley wrinkled her nose against the smell, wondering what on earth he was doing here.

"Hey," he said, looking up at her with bleary eyes. "I know you."

"Yes," she sighed, crossing her arms over her chest. "You do know me. I guess you live here?"

He reached up with his free hand and scratched his head, looking puzzled for a moment. "I do, I think."

"Great," Kinsley muttered. Why hadn't she looked to see who was in the other flats before she had chosen this one? She knew Jarred was living in one temporarily, but never in her wildest thoughts would she have considered it was the one next to her. He was drunk and she should just close her door. He wasn't her problem and old enough to know what he was getting himself into. Besides, it wasn't like someone was going to come along and pick his pockets or anything. This was a secured building. She should just cover him up and go back to bed.

"Hey," he said, his word slurring a bit. "You're so lucky. My father likes you."

She sighed, his words tugging on her conscience. She knew that their relationship wasn't on the best of terms, but the way he'd said those words, like a wounded child, made her heart ache. "Come on, let's get you up."

"I don't want to stand up," he mumbled as she reached down to tug on his arm. "The world spins when I stand."

Kinsley held her breath against the whiff of whiskey. "I imagine if you didn't consume half the whiskey in all of London it wouldn't do that."

"I—I had to forget," he said as she was able to get him to his feet, sending both of them crashing into the door. She winced as her shoulder hit the door hard, righting them as best she could. "Where are your keys?" she asked.

He grinned, a bit lopsided and very endearing. "My 'ocket."

"I hope that was your pocket," she answered, reaching down with trembling fingers to touch his pants pocket lightly. Lord, the man was pure muscle. Locating a bulge in his front pocket, she reached in and grabbed his keys, pulling them out red faced. She had just felt up Jarred Maloney. Rachel just thought it was a big deal that he'd hit on her. She hadn't touched him like this. Kinsley inserted the key into the lock and threw open the door, forcing them both to walk in. Thank goodness the layout was the same and in no time she had found his bedroom, directly opposite of hers, a wall separating them. "I hope you don't have much company," she said softly as she stood in the doorway, his arm slung around her shoulders. His body was close, way too close for her not to notice the warmth that was emanating from him, the way he was so solid.

His arm was wrapped around her waist lightly, but she could feel the burn of his fingers through her thin nightgown and wrap, the way he made her flustered and nervous. "I 'ate him."

She looked up, seeing the clench of Jarred's jaw as he looked ahead. "Hate who?"

He looked down, seemingly surprised she was there. "My father. He's an ass."

"He's also my boss," she said, moving them forward toward the bed. She would get him in the bed and then leave and hope that he would not remember she was ever here.

"Sorry," he mumbled. "Hope he doesn't screw you over like he does me."

"Me neither," she answered. "Come on, let's get you into bed."

"He hates me," Jarred sighed as she got him over to the bed and started to push him down. His hand reached up and grabbed hers, holding it against his chest. Kinsley forgot to breathe at the warmth of the contact, the way his heart was pounding against her hand, and she looked up, seeing the sad look in his eyes.

"He doesn't hate you," she said softly, resisting the urge to brush back the lock of hair that had fallen over his forehead. "You're his son."

"I screwed up," he answered softly, focusing his eyes on hers. "Lost a deal. He swore he would never let a screw up in his company. Told me I was a lost cause. Just like my mother…"

She winced. She didn't know the whole story of Jarred's mother. "You do screw up a bit" Kinsley reminded him, thinking of all the pictures on the internet. She had, more than once, heard the outbursts sitting outside of Mr. Maloney's office about his son, how he'd gotten his lawyers involved when the pictures were, well, revealing. "But anyone can change Jarred."

"Yeah," Jarred breathed. "I can show him I'm not a screw up."

"That's right," Kinsley answered, attempting to pull her hand away from his. It was too much, him touching her like this. It made her think things that were not possible, reminded her of what she was missing in her life. Companionship. Love. A life in general. She was missing all of that. "You can prove him wrong starting tomorrow."

He chuckled. "When did you become so smart?"

She grinned, his words endearing. "I've always been smart."

"I bet," he murmured, making a turn to the right with his entire body, catching her off guard. Before Kinsley knew it, she was falling back and being thrown on the bed, Jarred's heavy form collapsing on hers. The initial contact made the air rush out of her body.

If she thought mere hand holding was sparks, this was like electricity. He was like a warm blanket and her body wanted nothing more than to curl up against him and soak up the warmth. His head laid against her chest, his breath warm on her bare skin just above her nightgown. *Oh hell.*

"So soft," he murmured against her breast.

The mere words made her nipple tighten considerably. Oh wow. She swallowed hard. She wasn't supposed to enjoy this. He wasn't supposed to make her … ache.

"I need to forget."

"Forget what Jarred?" she asked softly, her hand finding his hair and smoothing over it lightly. He sighed in contentment and she smiled. This was absurd and strangely hilarious.

"Forget how fucked up I am."

His words tore at her, no matter how slurred they were and Kinsley couldn't help but wonder what was wrong between him and his father. This was a side that she doubted anyone saw of Jarred and had he not been liquored up so much, she doubted anyone would.

Hadn't he been engaged a few months ago? How much of him had his ex seen? *You two are the same.* Kinsley was all work, all seriousness outside of Rachel and Jamison. She had to work to show emotion to anyone else.

She glided her fingers through his soft hair, and she could fell the beat of his heart against her stomach. She shouldn't be here. She shouldn't be allowing this, but she couldn't force herself to leave either. When his breathing grew deeper, Kinsley removed her hands from his hair and knew she had to go. His body was heavier now, which told her that Jarred had either fallen asleep or passed out, which meant whatever moments they had just shared were in the wind.

She wouldn't say anything of course, one reason being she didn't need for him to know she was right next door. What if he asked his father about it? That would be disaster. But more importantly, she didn't want to embarrass him.

She pushed him aside and slid out from under him, falling to the floor with a thud on her bottom. Jarred mumbled something but didn't stir as she picked herself off of the floor and stared down at his prone form. Damn, the man was gorgeous.

Long legs and broad shoulders, and he certainly filled out those jeans. Something pulled low in her belly. It had been a long, long time since anyone had touched her. Even if they were both wearing clothes. *No, do not read anything into this.* She just needed a good shag. Yeah, as if that was going to happen anytime soon.

"Sleep well," she whispered, backing out of the bedroom and pulling the keys out of the door before setting them on the table in the foyer, shutting the door behind her. The hallway was blessedly empty as she moved back into her own flat, pushing the door closed before leaning against it, her body still drumming with excitement and want.

Kinsley knew she would have to be careful to stay out of sight for the next couple of days while she was here. No one would ever believe her and she could only hope that Jarred didn't remember in the morning either.

7

JARRED

Jarred lifted his head and groaned, squinting as he read the red numbers on the clock at his bedside. It was just after eight in the morning and he couldn't help but wonder what had happened last night. Kinsley Wells's face popped into his mind and Jarred closed his eyes, trying to rehash the last few hours. Had she been in his apartment? He vaguely remembered her hovering over him, concern on her pretty face. Her body pressed up against his, her soft planes fitting nicely into his hard ones. Even now he could feel his cock began to swell at the thought of being that close to her.

"Bollocks," he muttered, sitting up in the bed and scrubbing his hand over his face. The aftereffects of the alcohol he'd consumed the night before were still affecting his memory, but there was no doubt that at some point last night, he'd been very, *very* close to Kinsley Wells. Jarred looked down, realizing for the first time that he was still fully clothed. Well, if something had happened, shagging had not been part of it.

Swinging over the side of the bed, Jarred gave himself a moment, the regret of what he couldn't remember burning in his throat. He should stop drinking. But the alcohol dulled the pain that he couldn't handle, that he didn't *want* to handle. It made him forget everything, feel like all was right in his world for a few hours. No one would understand why he did it and to them he wasn't anything but a drunken sod, a worthless SOB who was drinking his life away. He shouldn't care what other people thought about him, but lately Jarred was starting to.

With a deep breath, he forced himself to stand and fight against the dizziness as he made it out of his bedroom and down the hall where he could find the coffeepot. After hitting the button to get the damn thing started, Jarred opened the balcony door and stepped out, the crisp air easing the pounding of his head.

He was only out there a few seconds before a familiar voice sliced through the air, desperation in every word. "No, please you have to listen. I can't. You can't expect me to be able to come up with that kind of money on such short notice. Yes, I understand but I've been one of your best renters for years. Surely that has to count for something."

Jarred leaned over to see Kinsley next door, her back to him as she held her phone up to her ear. Encased in a tight pencil skirt and long sleeved shirt, she was pacing the length of the balcony barefoot, her hair hanging down her back, teased by the slight wind in the air. "I understand," she stated into the phone. "But I just need some more time. My tuition is due and if I don't pay that soon, they aren't going to let me continue. Please, just a month, that's all I'm asking."

Curious, Jarred leaned against the half wall that separated their balconies, wondering what her situation was. Well, that and why she was next door in one of the company flats. He knew she didn't live here because he'd never seen her here before. Plus, he wasn't so certain she could afford to even rent one of these places.

"Yes, I understand," she said again, resignation in her voice. "Two weeks. I'll work on it." He heard her click off and sigh before he moved away from the wall, unsure of how to start a conversation with her. They hadn't exactly gotten off on the right foot as of late. He needed to apologize to her for whatever went on last night and offer to help her out with her problem he'd just been privy to. They could both help each other out, but right now he had to just figure out a way to get her attention.

He didn't have to. She turned and froze, her eyes widening. "Mr. Maloney."

"Jarred," he corrected, with a smile. "Good morning Kinsley."

"I, um, good morning," she said, looking nervous. "What are you doing here?"

"I live here," he answered with a quick grin. "What are you doing here?"

She visibly swallowed, nervously brushing the lint off her skirt and avoiding his gaze. "I, you woke me up last night when you came in. You were drunk."

The disdain in her voice was evident to Jarred and he frowned. She clearly didn't approve of him drinking. Well, she would not understand why. No one would understand why and he didn't have to explain himself to anyone, not even his father. "I was having a fine time," he said finally.

"Apparently," she said with a snort. Kinsley looked up and their eyes met briefly before she looked away again, crossing her arms over her chest. "Next time, how about you make it into your flat?"

Jarred crossed his own arms over his chest. "Why? When I have you to carry me to bed?" He was goading her, but he liked seeing her riled up. It made her come alive, lose some of her stiffness even if she hated his guts.

That did her in. Her eyes flashed with anger and she took a step forward, pointing at him with her finger. "You are the reason I didn't sleep well last night. You are the reason

I am dreading my day today. How about do us all a favor and sod off."

Jarred opened his mouth to speak but she didn't give him the opportunity, walking back into her own flat and shutting the door soundly. Jarred waited for a moment before exhaling a breath, a smile coming across his face. There was that fire he enjoyed seeing on her. While any other man would thank his lucky stars that he didn't have to deal with such a woman, Jarred enjoyed it. She was a refreshing change in his life, one that he needed desperately. And, she was perfect for his dilemma and after overhearing her conversation just a few minutes ago, he had ammunition to get her to agree to help him. She needed money for something. For what, he didn't know. But it was enough. Besides, he was running out of time.

8

KINSLEY

The next night, Kinsley sat at the table, twirling her straw around in her drink with her chin resting in her hand. Not too far from her, Rachel was giggling as some random bloke was attempting to snatch one of the condoms attached to her shirt with his teeth. Thank goodness they weren't attached to her chest, but rather near her belly button. Kinsley couldn't understand why all the other girls in attendance thought it would be hilarious for the bride to be covered in condoms attached to her shirt with strips of tape, but for some reason Rachel was having a ball with it. Since they had walked into the pub, the group had been surrounded by men of all types, the bubbly cousin attracting all kinds of attention.

Though she was the maid of honor, Kinsley had hung back as much as she could. This really wasn't her scene. And she couldn't get her mind off everything else. Her calls with the landlord had not been as productive as she would like. He had told her repeatedly that his hands were tied. Either she came up with the money or she was gone, as simple as that. There was no way she could come up with that kind of money, no way.

A loud cheer went up and Kinsley turned her head in time to see the lucky bloke with a condom between his teeth, giving Rachel a wink and then a hug as the women giggled around her. Another condom, another bloke who would go home tonight alone. What did they think a condom was going to get them anyway?

The bloke called for a round of shots and Kinsley rolled her eyes. Well maybe he thought if he got them all drunk enough, they all would go home with him. Fat chance at that. Jarred Maloney's face popped into her mind and Kinsley frowned. She wondered if he even remembered the other night when she had attempted to help him out. There were parts of that brief time in his flat that she hoped he didn't remember, like when she was running her fingers through his hair. That was an embarrassing moment on her end.

"Kinsley. Yoo-hoo."

Kinsley snapped out of her thoughts to find Rachel standing before her, a shot glass in her hand. "Here," she said, handing Kinsley the small glass. "It's tequila."

Kinsley looked at her friend, wearing a ridiculous pink veil and shirt covered with condoms and burst out into laughter. "You look ridiculous."

"I know," Rachel said with a shrug, her eyes already starting to glaze over from all the shots she had consumed. "But hey, I don't plan to ever get married again. I might as well enjoy this. Here take it and let's toast to my marriage."

"I'm so happy for you," Kinsley said as she took the glass. "I hope that you guys will be so happy together."

Tears appeared in Rachel's eyes as she leaned over and gave Kinsley a quick hug. "Thank you. I love you."

"Love you too," Kinsley said, a sudden rush of emotion flooding her and making her blink back tears. Her best friend was getting married, moving on with her life with her husband and Kinsley would become the third wheel officially.

Rachel straightened and held up the glass, Kinsley doing the same. "To love," she said before throwing back the tequila. Kinsley forced herself to do the same, shuddering as the liquid burned a path to her stomach. Rachel gave her a grin and turned back to the group of women behind her, leaving Kinsley to put her glass on the table and then stand. She needed to go to the loo.

Kinsley walked slowly toward the bathroom, her body starting to feel the effects of the liquor. She would have a raging headache in the morning, but luckily it was her day off. There wasn't much she was planning on doing, now that it looked like she was going to have to likely quit her lessons for now. The flats she had checked out today were twice as much as she was paying currently and even if she was forced to move out, all her money would have to go toward rent if she wanted to avoid moving in with her aunt and uncle again.

"Kinsley."

Kinsley turned around to find Jarred standing near her, and her heart immediately tripped as she took in his casual appearance. He was dressed in a shirt that matched his eyes, with a pair of low slung jeans and black leather jacket to ward off the cool night air. She was pleased to see that his gaze was sharp and clear, not muddied by alcohol. "Mr. Maloney," she said coolly.

He looked at her shirt and grinned. "Maid of honor huh?"

Kinsley looked down at the sparkly writing that spelled out her duties to the wedding party, glad that she wasn't the one that was covered in condoms. "It's Rachel's bachelorette party. I, *we*, are celebrating." She didn't know why she even needed to explain it to him. "Excuse me, I need to go to the loo."

She turned back to continue down the hall before his hand landed on her arm, the warmth of his skin on hers sending a shiver down her spine. "No wait," he said. "I need to talk with you."

Kinsley turned and found Jarred mere inches away from her now, close enough for her to see the tiny gold flecks in his emerald eyes. He smelled heavenly, the spicy scent of his cologne weaving its way around her. "W-what?" she forced out, her tongue seemingly not wanting to work.

Jarred leaned forward, until Kinsley was backed up against the wall, his arm resting just above her head. "Talk. We need to talk. I want to apologize for the other night. I was well pissed and appreciate you helping me out."

"I— you're welcome," she replied, wetting her lips with her tongue. Her pulse was racing, goosebumps breaking out over her skin. His eyes darkened and for a moment, a brief moment, Kinsley wondered what it would be like for him to kiss her. She had yet to forget the way his hard body had pressed up against hers the other night, the shocking contact still sizzling in her veins. It had been way too long since anyone had touched her. She wasn't starting with the boss's son. "Excuse me."

"I have a solution to your issue," he said softly, his eyes searching hers.

A wash of embarrassment fell over her, thinking of the conversation he heard on the balcony yesterday. She didn't want his help; she didn't need him to think that she couldn't handle her own issues. "No thank you," Kinsley said firmly, attempting to dip under his arm and escape. He moved his arm to block her attempt and she let out a groan in frustration.

"Listen," he said, urgency in his voice. "It'll be helping both of us out. I find myself in a situation that you can help me out in and in return I'll give you the money you need. That is all."

Kinsley looked up at him. "What kind of situation?"

His expression turned to one of embarrassment as he looked away. "I, um, I am in need of a fiancée."

That wasn't what she had expected him to say. The great Jarred Maloney needed to ask for someone to be his fiancée? Why in the world was he asking her? He could literally have any girl. One word and their knickers would wet with anticipation at the thought of even being close to the man. "You're kidding," she said, laughing. It was comical, really.

He looked back at her, his gaze narrowing. "No, I'm not. My father has given me an ultimatum regarding my trust fund and unless I bring a woman that can impress him, he's cutting me off. You're perfect."

His words reminded Kinsley of the other day, when he'd said that exact same phrase to her. Sure, he'd been pissed or hung over, but now she understood what they meant. How long had he been thinking about her helping him out? Wasn't he surprised that she was currently living next door, desperate for money? It had to be like a dream come true for him. "Why me?" she asked, unable to help herself. No way was she entertaining this plan. But she wasn't stupid, maybe he had a legitimate way to help her.

If she was going to agree to this fool plan, she wanted to hear it from his own lips why he chose to pick her over all the other willing women he could pick.

Jarred cleared his throat, her question obviously making him uncomfortable. "You're levelheaded," he started out. "My father already knows your character and trusts you. You are the opposite of what he would expect from me."

His words tore at Kinsley, not because he didn't mention her beauty. It was the way he said the last few words, like he was resigned to the fact that he was always going to be a screw up, the black sheep of the family. There was a hint of desperation in those words. "How much?" she forced out, wanting to shove away from the swell of emotions that she was feeling for Jarred at this moment.

Jarred's easygoing grin appeared on his face, though his eyes were still haunted with shadows as he looked at her. "600,000 pounds."

Kinsley's eyes widened. "What did you just say?" She hadn't heard him right. There was no way she had heard that amount correct.

"600, 000," he repeated. "No qualms, no payments. I'll give you the entire amount as soon as I am assured that my trust fund has been restored."

That was more than enough to buy the flat and finish school. More than enough to secure her entire future. The thought was dizzying. Kinsley swallowed hard, knowing she would be an idiot to turn the offer down. That money would solve all her problems and leave her comfortable for a quite a while. She could even afford to take a bloody vacation. Wouldn't it be nice to go somewhere for once? The choices of how she spent the money would be endless. More importantly, she could keep her life as it was, the life she knew. And she could finish school. That was the most important thing. On her own. Well, sort of. But what exactly would she have to do to get that dream?

"Think about it," Jarred said, pushing away from the wall. "I need to know by tomorrow."

Kinsley stared as he walked down the hall and disappeared around the corner, her knees weak from not only what he'd proposed, but also his closeness. Become Jarred Maloney's fiancée? He was her boss's son.

There were so many problems with that alone. What would she be required to do to prove that she was madly in love with him? How would they be able to pull that off, considering she was in his father's presence five out of the seven days of the week? Wouldn't he be suspicious? Or was

Jarred correct in his thinking that Mr. Maloney would never expect her to be with his son?

"Oh shit," she breathed. Was this seriously happening? She had to take the chance. How could she not? The more important question was going to be how she was going to survive in his presence. Because that weak-kneed, too hot feeling wasn't working for her.

9

JARRED

Jarred drew in a deep breath before opening the door, grinning as he spied Kinsley standing there. "Hey," he said, stepping aside. "Come in."

She stepped over the threshold and shifted her gaze around. After their discussion at the pub last night, he knew she would be coming over. The money alone was enough to draw her in. Jarred knew she needed the money and it was the perfect opportunity to solve both of their problems. "Come on in," he said, walking down the hall into the open living space. "Would you like some coffee?"

She shook her head, her long tresses falling about her shoulders. He noticed that she was wearing all black today, right down to the shoes on her feet and wondered if this was just a coincidence or symbolic. "I'm going to take the offer."

"I'm glad," he said, surprised that he meant it. She was going to be perfect. Kinsley tucked a strand of hair behind her ear and looked at him, giving him a small smile. He tamped down the quick flare of emotion. He hated the way a singular word could trigger those emotions, making him fucking weak. "You'll be fine," he forced out. "This will be easy."

She nodded and looked around the flat, avoiding looking at him. "So what should we do now?"

Jarred reached into his pocket, pulling out the ring he'd purchased late last night. He knew as soon as he'd left the pub that she was going to take the offer so he'd made arrangements to pick out a suitable ring to prove to everyone that she was truly his fiancée. The task had been harder than he'd realized, not knowing much about her. While picking out Susan's ring had been easy, given the fact she was a flashy person, he doubted the same could be said of Kinsley. In fact, he'd been in the jewelry store for well over an hour with just the owner present. Jarred cleared his throat and opened the box, his pulse pounding in his ears. "Um, Kinsley?"

She turned and her hands flew up to her mouth. Surprise registering on her face. For a moment, he was struck by how pretty she was. Not in an obvious way. So many people probably overlooked her because she was so understated. But the way her eyes widened as she looked at the ring and the way she conveyed emotion with her whole face, completely fascinated him. He wanted her approval; he wanted to impress her. This wasn't a woman he knew well, but she was a woman he didn't want to disappoint. All his carefully planned words would not form on his tongue as he held up the box. "Here," he forced out.

The surprise dimmed on her face and Jarred cursed inwardly. Shit. This thing wasn't real, but he did need her to like him. He'd fucking botched this. He needed her and he was fucking up.

Eventually, they would go their separate ways, but what bothered him the most was that she was going to remember this proposal long after she remembered him. Pissed off at himself, he pulled the ring out of the box and threw the box on the table, his grip suddenly slick. His fingers lost its hold on the ring and the ring fell from his hands. Immediately, he went down to retrieve it, his head colliding with something hard in the process and knocking him on his ass. Looking up, he saw that Kinsley was on the floor as well, rubbing her forehead with a wince. "Ouch," she said, sitting back on her knees.

Jarred laughed, because he didn't know what else to do and took her hand in his. "Probably not what you expected when you came over here this morning," he muttered.

She giggled. "No, not exactly. I think you are sitting on it."

Jarred found the ring under his thigh and held it up, the diamond sparkling in the morning light. "I don't really know what to say," he admitted, poising it over her ring finger. "This is not a conventional engagement, but I'll say this. As long as you wear this ring, I'll be devoted to you." She was helping him out in the biggest way possible and the least he could do was promise her that.

Her cheeks flushed and she nodded, giving him the out to slide the ring on her finger. "It's beautiful," she said softly.

Jarred cleared his throat, his thumb caressing the tips of her fingers lightly. The ring suited her, the petite emerald cut with smaller diamonds along the side of the band. It wasn't overly flashy but subtly beautiful, like her. He looked up and saw that she was watching him, her mouth parted slightly. He could kiss her. He should probably kiss her. But somehow, Jarred knew it wouldn't stop with one kiss.

Kinsley was the one who broke the moment, pulling her hand out of his and standing. Jarred followed suit and they looked at each other awkwardly. "What's the next step?" she asked, clasping her hands in front of her.

Jarred shoved a hand through his hair, frustrated at how the morning had went. He had planned this out in his head last night and it hadn't looked like this at all. "We have dinner with my father tomorrow night. We need to come up with a plausible story on how we met and how long we have been dating. He will be surprised to see you there."

"I agree," she answered. "How about the summertime? We can say we met at the company picnic."

"Did I attend the company picnic?" Jarred asked, not conjuring up that memory.

Kinsley pursed her lips. "No, I don't think so, but neither did your father. Is that, I mean, was that after your other engagement?"

Jarred winced as a stab of pain shot through his gut. Bloody hell, when would that pain ever go away? "Yeah, it was after that."

"Okay good," she said hastily. "So company picnic it is."

He nodded. "And we have kept it a secret because you didn't want to be drawn into the limelight."

"Yes," Kinsley answered. "That is plausible. You can say the rumors of other women were just a way to draw the spotlight off our relationship. You don't have photo evidence of other women right? That will kill this thing in the water."

He winced. "Maybe. But most of my shit has been under wraps. Most of the stuff the paps have caught has been of me drunk. But there will be rumors …" He cleared his voice. "Lots of them.

"I should go," she finally said. "Or I'll be late to work."

He nodded and walked her to the door, turmoil in his gut. "I—thank you for doing this," he said as she stepped out into the hallway. "You don't know how much you are helping me out."

"We are both getting something out of this," Kinsley answered. "It'll be fine."

Jarred started to say something else but closed his mouth and watched as Kinsley gave him a little wave, disappearing into the flat next to him. He was going to have to prove to his father that Kinsley was the love of his life. So why did that thought both excite and worry him? Bloody hell, he needed a drink and probably a psychological evaluation while he was at it. This plan was crazy as hell. But for the duration, he was laying off the booze. He needed a sharp mind to deal with this.

10

KINSLEY

This was crazy. Kinsley looked at the bed covered with four types of dresses, some borrowed from Rachel, and wished that she could just back out of this whole deal. She couldn't do this. Mr. Maloney was never going to believe that she was Jarred's fiancée.

"I like the yellow one," Rachel said as she sat on the bed, fingering the soft silk of the yellow wrap around Kinsley had just tried on. "It really makes your features pop."

"I can't do this," Kinsley blurted out, overwhelmed. "He's going to see right through this farce of an engagement and I'll lose my job."

Rachel gave her a sympathetic look. "Oh Kinsley, if anyone can do this, you can. Besides, think about the money. If I could do it, I would. It's Jarred Maloney."

Kinsley fell on the bed, rubbing her hand over her face. The diamond ring glittered in the light and she paused to look at it. Never in her life would she have thought she would be wearing a diamond like this. Or be engaged to Jarred Maloney of all people. She had thought about the day when she would meet someone special and wear a ring to signify their love but this ring, it didn't feel the same for obvious reasons. With a sigh, she picked up the yellow dress. "I think it's going to be this one."

"Kinsley," Rachel said softly, laying a hand on her arm. "I know this is going to be difficult and I'm here for you, regardless of what you decide. Maybe the money isn't worth it. Maybe you should back out."

Kinsley thought about the things she could do with that kind of money and shook her head. It would get her out of debt, help her never to worry about paying rent or whether she was going to finish her degree. With the money that Jarred was offering, she could forget it all. The weight would be lifted off her shoulders and maybe she could concentrate on her future, including her love life. Why was she having such a conscience about this? After all, it was Jarred that was deceiving his father and if she were sacked because of this, well, she was going to have enough money to float her until she could find another job. She could keep her carefully built life, the life she was comfortable with, by helping Jarred Maloney. It was far more than just money to her. It was her life, her future, and Kinsley was determined to ensure it all.

"Well I'm off," Rachel announced as she climbed off the bed and grabbed her purse. "Don't forget to pick up your bridesmaid dress from the tailor."

"I won't," Kinsley replied, looking at the clock. She had two hours to get ready for the night of her life. "I'll call you."

"You so better," Rachel said, giving her a little wave before disappearing down the hall. Kinsley waited until she heard the front door close before she climbed off the bed as well, picking up the yellow dress with a frown. It was too cheery. She wanted to look sleek, sophisticated and more importantly, look like she belonged on the arm of a billionaire. Putting the dress down, she picked up the black one instead. It was very unlike anything she would wear, one of the dresses that Rachel had brought over with her. Kinsley had dismissed it immediately, but now she knew she would wear it. With the right heels and jewelry, she could achieve the look she wanted.

Two hours later, Kinsley smoothed down the front of the dress, grateful for the shawl she had draped around her shoulders as she knocked on Jarred's door. Tomorrow she would go back to her own flat as the fumigation was complete and hopefully own the place before the end of the month. But first, she had get through this night.

The door opened and she took in the dressy attire of Jarred, glad that she went with the black. "Wow," he said as he stared. Leaning against the doorway with a grin on his handsome face, he muttered "You look great."

"I—thanks," she said nervously, feeling more exposed than great. The dress was a decent length, but the scoop neck had her boobs on display and no matter how much she adjusted, they were just there. She had left her hair down and applied minimal makeup, the shawl more of a cover-up than an accessory. "You look nice."

He gave her a grin and pulled his door shut. "You ready?"

"As ready as I am going to be," she admitted. They walked down the hall to the lift, Jarred pressing the button to call it to their floor before turning toward her. "You will be fine Kinsley. You're a natural. My father will love you. I mean, he already does. You just have to convince him you love me too."

"I hope he remembers that when he's evaluating my job," she joked. Jarred reached down and took her hand in his, the air sizzling around them as their bare palms connected. "Just breathe Kinsley," he said right above her ear, his breath ruffling her hair. "And trust me."

She nodded jerkily, her pulse pounding in her ears as the doors to the lift opened and they walked in. Jarred let go of her hand and she forced herself to breathe as he pushed for the garage and the lift started down. She could do this.

The doors opened and he led her to a sleek car parked in the garage. "Is this yours?" she asked as he opened the door for her. The car itself probably cost more than she would make in her lifetime.

"It is," he said as Kinsley climbed into the leather interior and he shut the door. She rearranged her dress and fumbled with her seatbelt as Jarred climbed in, shutting his own door and gunning the engine. He looked over at her and she gave him a smile, a flutter of nerves in her stomach. "Let's do this."

He nodded and they shot out of the garage and onto the dark streets of London. "Is there anything else I need to know about your father?" Kinsley asked, figuring she would use the ride time to prepare.

"Other than he's a bastard?" Jarred asked with a chuckle. "No, you probably know him better than I even know him."

Kinsley shook her head. "We rarely talk personally. Your father is all business, all the time." He was a good employer though, giving her a nice bonus around the holiday time and time off when she needed it.

"That doesn't surprise me," Jarred said as he turned down a long, winding road heading out of the city. "He's not a very touchy feely type person."

Kinsley wanted to say the same for the man next to her but kept her mouth shut. After all, they were to be a couple in love, not one that was fighting. "If you could be anything in the world, what would it be?" she asked instead.

Jarred's jaw clenched as he sped up the car. "You mean besides the loser my father and everyone else thinks I am?"

"Well you haven't helped out your cause," she reminded him gently. "Come on, humor me. What would you do?"

He sighed loudly. "I don't know, maybe be a professional rugby player. Honestly, I'd probably be a driver for the racing team."

Kinsley tried to picture Jarred as one of the brawny players she liked to watch on TV and shook her head. Well, he was handsome enough to be one. Or even more likely she could see him as a driver for the company's team.

"What about you?" he asked, his eyes on the road. "What would you be?"

"I think a world traveler," Kinsley replied with a heartfelt sigh. She would love to have enough money to go on holidays all the time. "You know, see other places, other cultures and blog about them. I think that would be the ultimate job."

"Someone has to suffer through that I guess," Jarred chuckled.1 "It might as well be you."

They fell silent as Jarred turned into a gated driveway, the gates thrown open to allow the cars to enter. Cars were already lining the drive as Jarred maneuvered into an open spot, shutting off the engine. "This isn't going to be a fun night," he said sharply, looking over at Kinsley. "I wish I could tell you differently, but I have no idea what my father is going to say or do, so just bear with it, okay?"

"Hey," Kinsley started, laying a hand on his shoulder. "I'm tougher than I look. I work for your father remember?" She wasn't scared of Mr. Maloney. Intimidated, yes, but she wasn't going to tell Jarred that. She felt, well, she wasn't exactly sure what she felt about the man next to her. He was hurting but put on one hell of a show, but he was hurting.

He nodded but didn't speak as they climbed out of the car, Kinsley taking a few deep breaths as they walked up to the massive brick house. It was gorgeous and far more expensive than probably her flat was. Every window was lit up on the inside and a man stood at the entrance, dressed in full butler attire as they reached the doorway.

"Master Maloney," he said as they walked into the interior of the house. "It's good to see you."

"You too Timms," Jarred replied, a rare true smile on his lips. "You're looking good."

"Thank you sir," Timms said, with a slight bow. "Your father and his guests are in the dining room."

Jarred nodded, his smile fading as Kinsley hurried to his side, grasping his hand. He looked over at her and she smiled, giving him false courage that she didn't even have. They were going to get through this night and she was going to be the best damn fiancée she could be.

Jarred started down the hall and she struggled to keep his pace, feeling the rigidity of his body in his grip on her hand. What was the big deal between him and his father anyway? Was this really about Jarred not living up to his father's expectations or was there something else? Something deeper? Kinsley was dying to find out.

They walked into the dining room and she was momentarily taken aback by its sheer size, as well as the extremely long table down the center of the room. All around the room were portraits of what she could only describe as ancient ancestors in gilt frames, not a one of them smiling. The room's colors were dark as well, giving a whole not so friendly vibe to the room itself. Great, not exactly where she would have expected to have to put on the performance of a lifetime. Her boss was standing near the sideboard as they walked in, hand and hand, his smile going to that of confusion and surprise immediately.

"Jarred," he said, the other guests all turning to view their arrival as well. "And Ms. Wells. This is a surprise."

"Dad," Jarred said tightly, his grip becoming tight on Kinsley's hand. She tried to keep a smile on her face and look like a woman in love, but doubted it was coming across that way to the guests. "This is Kinsley."

"Yes, I know," Mr. Maloney said, arching a brow at Kinsley. "I have to say I am surprised to see you together. My assistant never crossed my mind when you said you had met someone."

Kinsley felt Jarred release her hand and put his arm around her waist instead, pulling her against him gently. She felt the small electric thrill run down her spine at the closeness, thinking about how his body had covered hers the other night when he was pissed. "It's more than that Dad," Jarred said, a grin slowly covering his face. "We're engaged."

A gasp went up in the room as Kinsley laid her head on his shoulder, wanting it to look as if they were a couple in love. If anyone in this room was going to believe that they were really engaged, then she was going to have to play this up a bit.

"Well," a striking blonde in a tight red dress announced, her lips pursed. She was standing near the cart where the alcohol was, a champagne glass in her hand. "This is quite a surprise. I would have never guessed you to move on so quickly Jarred."

"What, like you Susan?" Jarred said, his gaze narrowing. Kinsley realized that this was the ex-fiancée, the woman who had left Jarred a few months ago. Rachel had been all over that gossip when it happened. From what Kinsley remembered, Susan was from a wealthy family and it hadn't been a surprise when the two had hooked up.

After all, they moved in the same social circles and their families knew each other. She was really beautiful and Kinsley was feeling a bit intimidated at the fact that Jarred's ex was now going to be a person they were going to have fool tonight. They had lived together, perhaps loved each other. She was going to sniff out the fraud in a hot minute if Kinsley couldn't play this up well enough. It wasn't the fact that she would lose the money, but more about the embarrassment for both of them. After all, she could lose her job over this given how pissed off her boss was if the word got out that they had played this up. Not only that, Jarred could stand to lose his inheritance.

Susan laughed lightly as a tall dark haired man came to stand behind her, his hand possessively on her hip. "Jealous Maloney?"

"Not in the slightest," Jarred laughed, his hand rubbing Kinsley's hip invitingly. "I wish you a very happy future, both of you."

"Hear, hear," Mr. Maloney broke in, lifted his brandy glass. "Congratulations to you all. This dinner has become a celebration of sorts. Come on in, let me introduce your lovely fiancée around Jarred."

Jarred's hand did not leave Kinsley's waist as he escorted her deeper into the room, where she greeted all the guests. The names started to run together and when they arrived in front of Susan and her new husband, the elder Maloney laughed. "Well I guess I don't need to introduce you," he said with a chuckle. "Can we play nice tonight?"

"Of course Harrison," Susan said smoothly, looking at Kinsley with a curious expression. "After all, we have always been like family. Isn't that right Jarred?"

Kinsley wasted no time leaning into Jarred's touch, a playful smile on her face as she looked up at him. "I can't wait to be a part of your family. It can't come soon enough."

Jarred looked down at her, his expression intense and Kinsley sucked in a breath, feeling the heat all the way to her toes. He was looking at her like he wanted to devour her and Kinsley couldn't help but wonder what would happen if this was real. Did people really have this soul searing intensity between them? She had never experienced it before, though she had seen the look pass between Rachel and Jamison a time or two. But from Jarred, she could melt into the wooden floor any moment. Though the little voice in the back of her mind told her this wasn't real, she couldn't help but wish it was. He leaned down, his lips brushing her cheek. "I can't wait to make you mine," he said softly.

Kinsley's pulse raced as a wave of longing and need pulsed through her. Everything would be so much easier if she wasn't this attracted to him. Somehow she doubted any other man would affect her the way that he did.

"Well," Mr. Maloney said as Jarred straightened. Kinsley swallowed and looked back at her boss, seeing a wide smile on his face. *He believed them.* Based on the frown on Susan's face, she was starting to believe as well. This was working. "Let's all sit down to dinner. I would love to learn more about how the two of you met."

11

JARRED

Jarred leaned back in his chair, his arm draped over the back of Kinsley's chair, his fingers barely grazing the back of her neck. They had finished the first course of his father's famous seven course meal, a long drawn out affair as a nod to the previous generations. He couldn't believe how well this was working out so far, but more importantly, he couldn't keep his hands off Kinsley. Ever since she had touched him in the car, his fingers were itching to touch her in some way. While he wanted to say it was because he was attempting to prove to his father that he was madly in love with this woman beside him, Jarred knew that his thinking wasn't exactly the truth. He fucking wanted her.

"So Kinsley," his father said, steepling his fingers together over his empty plate and giving them both his best businesslike expression. "How did you and my son meet? I'll be the first to admit I never thought my assistant and my son had much chances at all to form a relationship."

Kinsley looked over at Jarred shyly, her eyes shining in the dim lighting. Jarred felt a jolt of need straight to his gut at the simple look she was giving him, like he was the best damn man on the planet. How was she doing this? "Mr. Maloney, we met at the company picnic. Jarred tripped over my basket, spilling all my food out of it and by way of apology, bought me lunch. Of course he was an outrageous flirt. But I found him endearing."

Jarred gave her a grin, mainly because he was pleased with his choice. Kinsley was going to rock this and the innocent expressions she could maintain was going to erase all doubt in his father or anyone else's minds.

"That sounds very odd of Jarred, except for the flirting part," Susan said from across the table, doubt in her voice. Bloody hell. Susan was the wild card that Jarred hadn't anticipated. She knew him better than anyone and she was right, it didn't sound like him at all.

"Odd yes," Kinsley continued as the salad course was brought out to the table. "I have to agree I was surprised as well. After all, Jarred does have a reputation in the tabloids, doesn't he?" Jarred watched as she reached over and touched his arm lightly, giving it a small squeeze. "I didn't know what kind of guy I was really going to find, but I'm glad that I took the chance."

Her expression was so genuine that she stole Jarred's breath away momentarily. She was beautiful and he wanted to suddenly be that guy she was describing. They were just words, but then again they cut deep. Had he ever been that type of guy?

"Well, I still think it's very sudden," Susan continued, looking at Jarred with some disdain. "After all, I would have expected him to not want to move on so suddenly after, well, you know."

Jarred wanted to explode into laughter, thinking that she was one to talk. Hell, she was married now.

"After what?" Kinsley asked innocently. "Oh. You mean after your engagement? I'm just glad you turned him loose. After all, I couldn't have found the man I love had he married you."

Holy fuck. Jarred stared, shell-shocked, the room suddenly quiet enough to hear a pin drop.

"Well," Susan said with a nervous laugh as she looked at her glowering husband. "Of course. The same could be said for myself. After all, I am much happier with Baron."

The look on Baron's face told Jarred that he was bored with the conversation while the rest of the table waited on bated breath. "Seems as if we both have gotten what we wanted then," Kinsley finally said, looking up at Jarred. "I'm so happy with Jarred. He's changed everything about my life."

That was an understatement. Jarred knew he'd turned her life upside down, but for the first time in his life, he was glad he had. Kinsley was holding her own, turning out to be far better at this than he'd anticipated. He almost felt as if he needed to give her more money for handling Susan the way she had tonight.

"Hear, hear," his father said, raising his glass. "You did good son, picking out this gem. Now young lady. I just wish I'd known earlier."

"When will the happy nuptials take place?" one of the other guests asked politely as everyone turned to their salads. "Have you chosen a date yet dear?"

Kinsley laughed lightly and looked at the woman, giving her a warm smile. "Well, we want it to be a low-key affair so we were going to elope."

Jarred grinned. Damn, she was good. No fuss, no worries on the pressure of when they were going to actually get married.

"Absolutely not," his father said, frowning. "Every generation of Maloney has gotten married on this property dating back to the 1600's. My son will as well."

"Don't you think it's time to break tradition?" Jarred asked, looking his father in the eye. "This is our wish."

His father shook his head. "No Jarred. You are my only son. You will get married at the estate, end of story."

Jarred blew out a breath and started to object before Kinsley touched his thigh under the table. "Of course," she said. "I would hate to break tradition. Jarred and I'll need to discuss this if you don't mind."

"There's a level-headed woman," his father chuckled, picking up his fork. "She'll be good for you son."

Jarred said nothing, Kinsley's hand on his thigh having him think of all the things she could do to him under this table. His body felt like it was on fire, his pulse pounding in his ears and he silently urged her to move her hand upward, to his aching cock. One touch and he could very well explode. She was having an effect on him, one that he wasn't quite sure he completely understood.

Despite the constant tease, the next few courses went well, the chatter at the table not directed at Jarred or his farce of a relationship. He watched as Kinsley charmed the table, Susan glowering on the other side because she wasn't the center of attention. Jarred hated to admit it, but he was fucking glad that she wasn't. What had he ever seen in her to begin with? Kinsley was much more than she could ever be.

When the dessert course came out, his father rose from his seat, his glass high in the air. "I can't begin to explain how much my heart is warmed by the sight of my son finally happy with a beautiful, intelligent woman. I wish you both many years of happiness."

Kinsley looked back at Jarred and he tipped his glass toward her, his eyes silently thanking her repeatedly. They had done it. She had single handedly won over his father in a matter of hours. He doubted anyone else would have done the same.

"Kiss. Kiss." The chant rose up from the table, followed by laughter as the alcohol started to take effect. Kinsley's eyes widened slightly and Jarred looked around the table, seeing the glee in Susan's eyes. She didn't expect it to happen. Well damn, he was going to prove her wrong. With his hand, he cupped Kinsley's cheek, the softness of her skin in sharp contrast to his own. Her breath quickened as he leaned forward, his lips brushing hers ever so lightly before he devoured her with his mouth, tasting the champagne on her lips. She gasped against his lips and his tongue swept in, the rage of need flooding his veins. He couldn't get enough of her, her taste intoxicating.

When he heard someone clear his or her throat, he pulled back. What the hell had just happened? For several moments, he and Kinsley had been locked in a cocoon of lust and need and heat.

He focused his gaze on her flushed face and red lips. For a second, he considered apologizing, but couldn't get the words to form on his tongue. He wasn't sorry. Hell, he wanted more, much more.

12

KINSLEY

Kinsley gave Mr. Maloney a smile as he escorted them to the door, glad for the moment when she could take a deep breath and consider her job done. Her nerves were scattered, especially after the searing kiss Jarred had given her.

"I expect you will no longer want to be my assistant," her boss was saying as Jarred opened the front door. "Which I'm not sure I could have my soon-to-be daughter-in-law working fetching me coffee."

"Oh no," Kinsley said abruptly, frantically looking at Jarred. She could not lose her job. "And sir, I don't actually fetch you coffee. One of the admins does that. I just make sure the kind you like is there when you arrive." She doubted he knew just what her job was as his Executive Assistant.

"I'm sure Kinsley will still like to work for now father," Jarred interjected, wrapping his arm around Kinsley's waist. "If you will allow her to have some time to help me with my work at the company."

"Of course, of course," her boss replied, giving them a smile. Kinsley saw no malice, no falsehood in his expression, telling her that Jarred's father was clearly happy that they were engaged. The thought didn't sit well with her. She'd known what she was getting into, but now that they had accomplished their goal, the lies tore at her. She liked him. She didn't want to lie to him. "Then I shall see you tomorrow Kinsley."

"Yes sir," she forced out and followed Jarred outside into the cool night.

They made it to the car before Jarred let out a large breath. "You were fucking awesome tonight," he said.

"I, thanks," she answered, fidgeting with her clutch. "I hope I didn't overstep any boundaries or anything." Susan had pissed her off to no end. Where the courage came from to do so, she had no idea.

"God no," he said, glancing over at her with a smile on his handsome face. "You handled Susan better than I ever could. You should be an actress."

Kinsley gave him a halfhearted smile, wishing she could relish in the fact that she had performed great tonight. But the touches, that kiss, they had been far more than just acting. Throughout dinner she had wondered what it would be like to be with him, to have him constantly *wanting* to touch her instead of pretending. He was charming, devilishly handsome, every girl's naughty fantasy and for a very short while, he was hers. How was she going to handle it when this was over? That was the problem with pretending. It was way too easy with Jarred to get attached. And what if he kissed her again? What if things went beyond kissing? She couldn't handle it. It was hard enough to stay detached when they had shared a kiss or two. But shagging? Kinsley knew she would stand to have more to lose if they went down that path.

"We need to be seen out on the town," Jarred was saying as he drove them back to London. "A date."

"A date," Kinsley said slowly, the thought of being seen in public with Jarred both exciting and terrifying.

"Yeah," Jarred answered as he turned the car into the garage. "Dinner, drinks, whatever you want to do. I think it'll solidify what we started tonight."

Kinsley swallowed hard, worried. That would thrust her into the limelight and send tongues wagging. The paparazzi would attempt to find the dirt on her life. They would bother the people that raised her, hound Rachel during the most stressful time in her life. No. Kinsley couldn't allow that to happen. "I, no. I don't want to go on a date with you."

Jarred pulled the car into the parking spot and shut off the engine before looking over at her. "What?"

"I mean," Kinsley said quickly, "I'd rather keep this as quiet as possible. After all this is all a farce anyway. Can't we just keep up appearances for your father? And what happens when we break this off? I mean I'll be hounded and humiliated."

Jarred stared at her, his jaw clenched tightly and Kinsley fought the urge to touch him, knowing it wasn't what he was hoping for. After tonight, she was going to have a very hard time keeping her hands off him. "Fine," he finally said. "We will do it your way. Tonight worked so well so if we keep it up, there shouldn't be anything to worry about."

Kinsley nodded and looked away, drawing in a breath. "Good, as long as we are on the same page then."

"The same page," Jarred repeated. Kinsley opened her door and climbed out, Jarred following suit, mere inches between them. Kinsley bit her lip, thinking that she didn't know what page she was on truly. Her mind kept drifting back to that kiss, the one that had warmed her all the way to her toes and had her craving more. She shouldn't crave Jarred. It was all wrong to do so. He wasn't her type of guy, yet the more she learned about him, the more she liked him. They walked into the lift and Jarred shut the door, leaning against the side of the lift watching her. She looked over at him, wetting her lips in the process. "What?"

He shook his head slowly. "Nothing."

"I don't believe you," Kinsley said with a nervous laugh. She hoped that she didn't have anything on her face that would keep him looking.

He ran a hand through his hair roughly, looking slightly out of sorts. "I, uh, I should walk you up."

Kinsley laughed; she couldn't help it. "I live right next door."

"Right," Jarred said, a slow, sexy grin on his face. Kinsley's pulse fluttered and her face heated, wondering how someone could be so dangerous and sexy at the same time. "Things can happen on your short walk Kinsley."

She nervously clenched her hands together to keep from reaching out and touching him. "L-like what?"

Jarred pushed off of the wall and started to close the gap between them, causing Kinsley's breath to come out in short puffs. The look on his face was feral and her body was responding in thus. *She wanted him.* The thought hit her like a ton of bricks. Oh god, she shouldn't want him. He wasn't good for her. They wouldn't even be this close if she hadn't agreed in this fool plan to begin with.

He reached out and gently grasped her chin, his fingers warm on her skin and sending sizzling sparks throughout her body. She waited with bated breath for him to say something, do anything, the tension in her body tight as a drum. The lift dinged and they both fell apart. Kinsley cleared her throat as she walked down the hall, her body tingling in areas that hadn't tingled in quite some time. Bloody hell, he hadn't even really touched her and she was already melting into the floor. "Well, here we are," she said, her voice coming out tight as she stopped in front of her flat door.

Jarred leaned against the outside of the doorway, a slight smile on his face. "See? You need protection."

Kinsley looked down the hall, seeing no other person in sight. "I don't see anyone else."

He didn't answer, his eyes growing dark. "Maybe I was lying. Maybe I need to see if I am imagining this."

"I-Imaging what?" she asked, her voice shaking slightly.

"This," he answered right before his lips descended on hers. Kinsley felt the current of electricity on her lips, the heightened awareness of her own body as Jarred's lips molded against hers. She could smell his cologne swirling around her, the taste of him something exotic and forbidden. But she wanted more. She needed more. His tongue traced her bottom lip and she gasped, allowing him entrance to the inner recesses of her mouth. His tongue touched hers and Kinsley saw sparks, her hands blindly reaching out and grabbing his shirt to pull him closer. She was on fire and it was all because of Jarred.

Jarred's hands gripped her shoulders, sliding down her arms until his hands covered her breasts through the material of her dress, the laciness of her bra now becoming an erotic feeling against the rock-hard nubs of her nipples. Jarred's tongue was doing wonderful things in her mouth and Kinsley didn't want to pull away, instead leaning into his touch as his tongue stroked hers. His hands inched down to the hem of her dress and before Kinsley knew it, Jarred's hands were sliding up her bare thigh, touching the silkiness of her panties around her hip area. His hand was warm and she felt her own body flood with wetness at the thought of his hand sliding just a few inches and touching the very core of her. Her knees weakened as Jarred's hand started toward her aching center, the slowness of his hand filling her with agitation. She could just shift slightly and he would be there.

But before she could, he broke their kiss, his breath harsh against her cheek as he backed away. Kinsley stood there, feeling slightly embarrassed at the wantonness of her body, wanting to throw her arms around him and beg him to continue.

"I-I should go," he said, raking his hand through his hair. "Go inside."

"I," Kinsley started, her body throbbing with need. What was she going to do, ask him inside? Did she dare to do that?

"Good night," he said, stalking down the hall instead of opening his door. Kinsley watched him go, some of the heat dying down now that he was leaving her, panting with need. What had just happened?

Jarred

JARRED ENTERED the lift and waited until the doors were shut before he drew in a breath, his body rigid and heavy with need. He had almost shagged Kinsley in the fucking hall. Of all the stupid things he could do, that had to be at the top of the list. It would prove to her that he was the loser, the playboy everyone thought he was and she would regret ever helping him in the first place. He couldn't do that to Kinsley. He didn't want to do that to Kinsley. He wanted her to see him in a different light, maybe even the good guy that no one believed he could be. Stopping himself tonight had taken a feat of strength and self-control that he didn't know he had, but Jarred considered that most of that strength had come from his respect for Kinsley. She was much more than just a shag in the hallway. She deserved flowers, candlelight, a bed.

The lift doors opened and he walked out in the direction of his car, his mood black and his cock hard as a rock, demanding release. He had been so close to having her, to burying himself in her warmth. There was no way he could go to his flat knowing she was right next door, no doubt ready and willing. He had felt her need in her kiss and it was just as strong as his had been. No, it would only take a few steps for him to bang on her door and have his way with her, which was why he had to get out for a while. Where, he didn't know but it couldn't be here.

The next morning, Kinsley grabbed her suitcase and walked out of the flat, closing the door behind her. Her own flat was now ready for her to move back in, which was a relief, and with the money she would get from Jarred in a few days, she could make the entire payment to make the place hers. The feeling was beyond explanation and would have been enough for her to go back, but now, she needed space from Jarred. After last night, Kinsley knew they were treading on dangerous ground, very dangerous ground. She still couldn't understand why he'd left her like that, when she would have gladly dragged him into bed for as long as he wanted to stay.

Stopping in front of his door, Kinsley took the piece of paper she had written on this morning and slipped it under the door before continuing to the lift. It was a short note, one that just told him she was going back to her own flat and the address where he could find her. Kinsley had not heard him come in last night and while she didn't want to think about him or his safety, the nagging voice in the back of her head told her she cared about her fake fiancée. She cared about whether he got back to his flat. She cared if he had gone home with another woman last night. It also terrified her. She would have slept with him last night if he hadn't stopped them. She'd been spinning in a spiral of lust.

"Buck up Wells," she said to herself as she pressed the button for the lift. Jarred wasn't her problem. They weren't even in a real relationship. He was paying her to be with him, not to worry about him. She was best served to keep that in her mind.

The lift arrived and Kinsley stepped inside, pressing the button for the ground floor. Her phone rang, causing her to fish it out of her bag. "Hello?"

"So, how did it go?"

Kinsley sighed into the phone, grateful that it was Rachel. "It went well. I think we pulled it off."

"How did he like the yellow dress?" Rachel asked, the sound of the tube in the background.

Kinsley smiled as the lift arrived at the ground floor and she stepped out. "I wore the black one."

There was a beat of silence. "Oh my," Rachel said, surprise in her voice. "I can't believe you wore that one. I thought you were going for demure."

Kinsley thought about why she wanted to wear the black dress. She had wanted to see that heated look in Jarred's eyes, to at least pretend that for a moment he wanted her. Mission accomplished. "I wanted to be sexy."

"Oh Kinsley," Rachel sighed. "You know I love you like a sister, so I am going to tell you to be careful with this one. He's way out of your league and will break your heart."

"I know," Kinsley said. Her cousins words rang true, but it stung that Rachel pointed out that she was nowhere in the league to be playing with billionaires. Hastily, she blurted out, "He kissed me last night." She was going to keep the rest to herself right now.

There was another pause. "God, I hate you now," Rachel laughed. "You were kissed by Jarred Maloney. How was it?"

"It was wonderful," Kinsley admitted as she walked down the sidewalk toward the tube that would take her home. It was irrelevant that they had been forced to do so. "His ex was there last night too."

"I need all the details later," Rachel said. "I gotta go, but drinks tomorrow? Don't forget to pick up your dress. I can't believe the wedding is so close."

"Me neither," Kinsley said before Rachel rang off. She wanted that excitement that her best friend was feeling, she wanted to feel as if she was the luckiest woman in the entire world.

With a sigh, Kinsley entered the station where the hustle and bustle of the morning was evident, the passengers hurrying to catch the tube that would take them to their destination. What destination was she looking for in her life? When she got the money, some of her worries would instantly disappear. But was that enough? Didn't she want to experience some of the love and affection that Rachel was experiencing in her life right now? Her best friend didn't know how lucky she was.

Jarred flitted through her mind and Kinsley pushed that thought of their fevered caresses aside. No way. Jarred wasn't the man for her. They were from two different worlds really. Plus, this was just for the money, wasn't it? He was a solution to her problem.

"What have I gotten myself into?" she muttered to herself, tapping her foot as the tube slowed to the station. No matter how much she tried to ignore it, this partnership of sorts was way more than just some money now. The problem was she didn't know how to handle Jarred ... or his kisses

13

JARRED

Jarred pulled his cell out of his pocket, looking down at the screen with a frown. His father's number flashed back at him, causing him some heartburn. Today he'd been working on the other half of his father's demands for his trust fund, visiting the headquarters for the Formula One team. Racing had always been something he was interested in; the excitement and adrenaline were a plus. But there was such a purity to the cars. He loved chatting with the engineers about how they tried to make the cars faster.

He'd dabbled a little in the actual business aspect of the team, but nowhere near enough to actually be in charge of it. Before, he'd been more of a hobbyist, sneaking off incognito to races to watch. Susan had hated anything to do with the racing so she'd refused to go. Add to it that he'd deliberately wanted to avoid publicity, and she really wasn't interested.

The more Jarred thought about it, the more he wondered how he'd been with her for so long. How he'd ever convinced himself that he loved her.

Now that his father was forcing his hand, he was finally getting to take an open interest in something he genuinely loved. Not that he was ever telling his father that. All morning he'd been meeting with various people within the headquarters, learning as much as he could. So far, he was actually enjoying himself. And the kicker was, he could actually be good at this.

His inner adrenaline junkie wished they'd stick him behind the wheel. He'd floated that idea, but of course the lawyers had all paled at the potential insurance cost. But maybe when he finally had his full trust fund, he'd be able to build a car just for himself.

Holding the phone to his ear, he pressed the button. "Hello, Father."

"Jarred," his father said. "I hear you are spending time with the racing team this morning. That's good son, very good."

"Just doing what you are requiring me to do," Jarred said. He was actually having fun learning the racing side of the company, but he wasn't going to tell his father that.

"I'm just trying to help you with your future Jarred," his father said, disapproval in his tone. "Surely you can see that."

"What do you want Dad?" Jarred sighed, not wanting to have this conversation *again*. He was going to play by his father's rules for now, but not for the rest of his life.

"I was thinking," his father started, "that maybe you and Kinsley should meet with a wedding planner. I have made some calls and have secured one of London's foremost wedding planners to help you with your wedding. She's willing to meet with you both today."

"Dad," Jarred warned, his mind scrambling at what he was going to say about this. This was when he needed Kinsley and her fast thinking to smooth this over. He hadn't seen her since last night, but she wasn't going to like this change of events. "Kinsley and I can handle our own wedding planning."

"I understand," his father said. "But I was thinking this weekend would be a perfect time to have the wedding. This planner, she's a gem and can plan whatever Kinsley likes. Money is no object. I'll be footing this bill, of course. Think of it as a wedding present. It's not every day my only son finds a woman he wants to wed."

Jarred rubbed a hand over his face. His father had lost it, truly. Didn't he have better things to do than just sit around and try to plan a wedding? What had gotten into him? "Don't you think that Kinsley should be able to plan this wedding? Isn't that what brides like to do?"

His father was silent on the other end for a few moments. "You're right of course," he finally said. "I'll talk with Kinsley. She will see the reasoning."

"Wait," Jarred said as his father rang off. Damn. Why did he have to be so pushy? His phone still in his hand, he walked outside where his car was parked, the dreary, overcast day matching his mood now. He needed to talk with Kinsley. Jarred dialed his father's office, impatience settling in his body. She was probably upset about him leaving so abruptly last night but after dinner and that kiss, he'd needed to get the hell away from her. Because one more moment in her presence, he'd have started to forget that shit wasn't real and he'd have made love to her repeatedly. Matter of fact, they'd both still be in bed. He'd have kept her in bed until she begged off from too many orgasms.

The problem was that last night, when he visited one of the clubs that he frequented on a regular basis, there was no joy in being there. He'd sat in the VIP section of the club, a drink in his hand and glowered. So angry at himself for needing to be exactly who his father thought he was. Angry with his father and everyone else under the sun for never believing in him.

But most of all, he missed Kinsley. Her touch, her voice, the way she had damn near charmed everyone at dinner, minus Susan. She had floored him, intrigued him, and made him want her worse than he already did.

"Mr. Maloney's office, may I help you?"

"Kinsley," he gritted out, his voice harsh in his own ears. "It's Jarred."

"Hi, um, Jarred," she answered, surprise in her voice. "Your father just stepped out."

"I don't want to talk to him," he said, attempting to control his anger. He wasn't mad at her; he was mad at himself. "I want to talk with you."

"Um okay," she said. "About what?"

"Tonight," he blurted out, a plan forming in his mind. "We need to get together tonight."

"Why?" she asked, the wariness apparent in her voice.

Jarred climbed in his car and started the engine. Should he be honest with her and tell her that he really just wanted to see her? It was the truth, no matter how he wanted to spin it. He missed her and it was fucking killing him. "My father called me. He wants us to get married this weekend."

She made a noise somewhere between a choked cough and laugh. "Oh, that's not going to happen," she said, nervousness in her voice. "I hope you told him so."

"If he asks about a wedding planner, tell him whatever it takes to stall," Jarred said, pulling out of the parking lot toward his flat. "And come over when you get off of work."

"You haven't been home have you?" she asked softly.

Jarred frowned. "Why?" He hadn't been home. He had spent the night at Turner's, who wasn't happy to be woken up at 2 a.m. but Jarred hadn't wanted to go home.

"I left you a note," she answered with a sigh. "I'm back at my place now. I left you the address in case you, well, if you needed me."

He grinned, just because she thought he needed her. Hell, he did need her. The realization was like a sucker punch to the gut. Damn, what had happened to him? "I'll come over. We can order out some food." She didn't answer right away. "Come on," he urged. "We need to spend time together to prove that we are a couple. I'll spring for whatever food you want."

"All right," she finally said. "I get off at five. You can come over at seven."

"See you then," he said, ringing off before she could change her mind. After running from her last night, he was going to run to her tonight and the thought was far more exciting than going to any club.

Jarred

JARRED ARRIVED RIGHT AT SEVEN, with flowers and a few bottles of a nice red wine, feeling like a teen going out on his first date. The flowers had been a last-minute thought, thinking that Kinsley would probably like them. What woman didn't? The address that she had provided in her note was an older building, one of the charming sections of London that still had some of the original structures, far removed from the modern buildings near the heart of the city. No wonder she wanted to stay in this area.

Walking up to the building, he located the lift and found himself in front of her door in no time, nerves mounting inside. His hands were bloody shaking. What was wrong with him? Disgusted with himself, he knocked on the door. It opened a moment later and Kinsley was standing before him, dressed in a simple T-shirt and leggings, her hair down around her shoulders.

"Hey," she said, giving him a little wave.

"Hey yourself," he said, presenting her with the flowers. "I got these for you."

"They are beautiful," she said softly, taking them from him and inhaling their scent. "Thank you. You didn't have to."

"I wanted to," Jarred responded, a grin on his face. The flowers had been a good call. "I brought wine too."

"Come in then," she said, stepping aside to let him pass. He briefly thought of kissing her, thinking that was what couples did. But they weren't really a couple and he wasn't sure how she would react. So instead, he just walked in, surprised by the colorful scene before him.

"I, welcome to my flat," she said behind him, her arms crossed over her chest. "I know it's vastly different from yours."

Jarred took in the brightly colored couch and chair, the mismatched furniture that somehow worked in the space and found that he liked here far better than the sterile feel of his father's company flat. He could see her personality in her living space. No wonder she wanted to save the place. "I like it," he said, turning toward her. She blushed and turned to the kitchen, taking a pitcher and arranging the flowers in it before setting them on the island.

"So your father didn't have a chance to talk to me today," she said as he set the wine on the counter. "He got wrapped up in some business issue and was out of the office the rest of the afternoon."

"That's good," Jarred replied. "It'll give us a chance to concoct a story for tomorrow. You blew him away Kinsley. He's infatuated with you."

She bit her lip and busied herself pulling down some wine glasses from the cabinet. Jarred opened the wine and poured them both a healthy glass, holding it up for a toast.

"To bright futures," he said. She clinked her glass against his and then took a large swallow.

"This is good," she said. "Good choice. I hope it wasn't too expensive."

He grinned, knowing now not to tell her exactly how much the wine cost. He doubted a few hundred pounds broke the bank, but it would embarrass Kinsley and that wasn't his intention. She took another sip before setting her glass on the island. "So, what's going to be our story?"

Jarred leaned against the island, his glass in his hands. "I don't know. Tell me about your dream wedding."

"Dream wedding?" she echoed, her eyes widening in surprise.

He nodded, knowing all women had planned out their entire future when they were, like, ten. "You know, what would you want it to look like?"

She took another healthy swallow of the wine, her brows knitting together. "I, wow, I don't know if I've thought about it."

Jarred laughed. "Surely you have thought about it. I thought all women had the shit like written down somewhere."

Kinsley laughed, her cheeks flushing from either his musings or the wine, he couldn't tell. "I've never written it down. I guess I just always thought it would fall into place. I really don't care about the wedding; it's more about the person."

As soon as she said it, she looked away. Jarred cleared his throat, feeling a bit like an ass for asking. He knew he wasn't ideal marriage material. Susan had been clear with him on that. He had pushed Kinsley into this, playing on her weakness, her need, and now he was trying to pry into her life.

"Well," she finally said, her glass now empty. "What about you? Have you ever thought about marriage?" As soon as the words were out of her mouth, she covered it, dawning horror on her face. "Oh, I'm sorry about that. I didn't mean anything."

Jarred held up his hand. "It's fine, really," he said, vaguely uncomfortable with the mention of his failed engagement. After last night, he was kind of glad his relationship with Susan had ended like it had. "I'm good with it."

Kinsley reached over and grabbed the wine bottle, pouring herself another glass. "I have to say, she's not your type."

Intrigued, Jarred drained his glass and poured the rest of the bottle in his glass. "What's my type Kinsley?"

She took a large swallow. "I don't know. Someone outgoing, able to put up with you."

Jarred laughed, thinking that she had danced around the question. She was his type currently; she just didn't know it. What he thought was going to be an uptight, hard assed woman had turned into someone he enjoyed spending time with. After all, he was here tonight, with a beautiful, lively woman he suddenly couldn't get enough of. "Well I don't need much then."

"Can I ask you a question?" she asked softly, her fingers playing with the stem of her glass and avoiding his gaze.

Jarred swallowed, a thousand thoughts of what her question could be running through his mind. "Sure."

"Why do you hate your father so much?"

The absolute worst fucking question she could ask. He would give her his bank account number over answering that question. "Why do you want to know?" he asked abruptly.

She looked at him then, her expression sympathetic. "I'm sorry. I shouldn't pry into your life like this. I just, I can't understand what has driven this rift between the two of you."

"I-I never live up to his expectations," Jarred finally said, the swell of disappointment building in his veins. He never did. No matter what he got involved in or the grades he made in school, nothing was enough to satisfy his overachieving father. More than once, Jarred had heard how he'd screwed up in his lifetime.

One day in particular stood out, when he'd overheard his father telling one of the board executives that his son would never amount to anything. "A loser," he'd called Jarred, laughter in his voice. "That's all he will ever be." The words had stung more than Jarred had anticipated. While he wasn't the son he knew his father wanted him to be, he wasn't a fucking loser either. After that, he just quit giving a shit about what his father thought of him. However, he never anticipated his father taking away his source of income and putting him in this situation. Bloody hell it sucked.

"I can never be the almighty Harrison Maloney. I don't want to be my father. I don't want to be my grandfather. I want to be me." He wanted to be happy in whatever he decided to do with his life.

"You're not your father," Kinsley said. He waited for the punchline, the ways she was going to tell him how he failed like everyone else liked to do, but she didn't. "And you shouldn't try to be. Jarred, you should find something that you are really good at, something that makes you happy and stick with it. Screw your father or whomever else tells you that you are a nobody."

Jarred watched the passion flare in Kinsley's eyes as she gave him a pep talk, the warmth spreading over him as well. She was quite a surprise. How had he not noticed her before now?

She looked away then, her cheeks flushing red and Jarred realized he was staring, making her uncomfortable. "That's good advice," he told her, not wanting to make her feel awkward. Maybe he needed to hear that from someone else, someone that barely knew him.

He watched as Kinsley finished her glass and reached for the other bottle, breaking open the seal before pouring another full glass. "So," she said as she sat the bottle on the counter. "What's going to be our story for your father?"

The real reason he was here. Jarred had forgotten all about it. "I don't know," he said slowly, sipping his wine. "Can't you just throw one of those fits about wanting to plan your own wedding?"

She laughed, a warmth in her eyes from the wine. "Do you really think that will work?"

Jarred shrugged, a grin on his face. "Hell, I don't know but it's worth a shot."

Kinsley giggled, cocking her head to the side. "You know, I would have never expected you to be so ..."

"So what?" Jarred asked, finding himself wanting her to finish the sentence. What did she see him like?

"So likeable," she said with a blush, drinking her wine nervously. "You're not the rich playboy I expected."

Jarred set his glass down, glad that she didn't think he was a snob or something. He never had been. If he had, then maybe he and his father would have gotten along better. Maybe he and Susan would be married now. A shudder went through his body at the thought of being married to someone like Susan. She had shown her true colors last night and Jarred couldn't help but be glad he'd dodged that bullet.

Kinsley took a few steps forward, until she was directly in front of him. He looked down at her, taking in her natural beauty without all of the makeup and shit that women liked to pile on. It was nice to see what was underneath. "I want to kiss you," she said suddenly, her tongue darting out to wet her pink lips.

Yes. Hell yes. Surprised at her boldness, Jarred forced himself to put on an easy grin, his thoughts scattering. Kiss him? She could kiss him whenever the hell she wanted to. "You can do whatever you want to me Kinsley." His cock twitched as if to say, "Yes, please."

She gave him a slight smile before reaching up, pressing her lips to his. Jarred felt the warmth of her skin touching his, the way her lips nibbled on his lips and felt the sudden rush of want enter his body, igniting him from the inside out. He wanted her, there was no doubt about that. Hell, his pants had never felt so tight before.

She deepened the kiss, her hands reaching out to touch his shoulders and Jarred took the opportunity to put his hands on her waist, drawing her until they were flush. She let out a small gasp and he swept in, plunging his tongue into her mouth. Her taste was intoxicating and he knew he wouldn't be able to get enough of it. Her hands clenched into his shoulders as he ravaged her mouth with his, his own grip tightening on her waist, waiting for the opportunity to move. Would she allow him to do that? When had he held back on what he did with a woman? But this was Kinsley, the woman that was saving his ass. She wasn't just any woman, not to him.

She pulled back and he allowed her to, seeing the dull flush of her cheeks, the redness of her lips from his kiss. "I think, I mean I *want*," she started, her words not coming out in complete sentences.

Jarred leaned down, his hands roaming up her back. "What do you want Kinsley?"

Her breath was warm against his cheek, rapid puffs of air that told him she was excited at what was transpiring between them. He sure was. He had the hard on to prove it. "I-I think I want you," she said softly, her words barely above a whisper.

Jarred chuckled, his hands coming to rest on her shoulders as he pulled back to look at her face. "You think or do you know?"

Kinsley chewed on her lower lip, refusing to meet his gaze. "I know," she said finally.

Thank the heavens above. Jarred grabbed her hand and pulled her to the couch, falling on it before pulling her down with him. Before she could even grasp what he was doing, he had her pinned under him, his upper torso covering hers. "I fucking want you," he said, emboldened by her own bold words. After their near fucking session last night, he was ready to get this party started with her. He would be good to her.

Her eyes widened and he covered her mouth with his, feeling her arms encircle his neck. She kissed him with abandon, her own tongue seeking out his and surprising the hell out of him. This was the woman he wasn't expecting. With his own hands, he slid under her shirt and cupped her breasts, still encased in a lacy bra. She arched against his touch as he found her erect nipples, rolling the points between his fingers. He was hard as a rock, the thought of having Kinsley naked under him nearly breaking him.

She pushed on his shoulders and he broke the kiss. "I-I-let me slip into something more comfortable," she said, killing the mood instantly. "I'm sorry."

"No worries," Jarred said, sliding off of her and standing. If she saw the tent that was in his pants, she said nothing, sliding off of the couch to a standing position and stumbling slightly as she walked down the hall. Jarred ran a hand through his hair roughly. Jesus, what was she doing to him? This was worse than when he was a teenager. Because he knew just how good she'd feel around him. He needed to take it slow. He didn't want to give Kinsley any reason to call this off. Hell, he might explode if she did.

He waited a few minutes before starting down the hall himself. Maybe she had decided to go ahead and climb in the bed. "Kinsley?" he asked as he located the bathroom, finding it empty. There was no way she could have escaped without him noticing. Walking into the bedroom, Jarred drew up short of the bed, finding Kinsley sprawled out on one side, still in her clothes. *Bloody hell.*

Had she really had that much wine? She'd had what? Two glasses? Maybe she didn't drink much. But either way, nothing was happening with them right now. He walked over to her and was relieved to see the rise and fall of her chest. She was going to have a devil of a headache in the morning.

Jarred looked at her, smiling as a soft snore escaped. He hated that their night had ended so abruptly. For one of the first times in his life, he'd actually been enjoying himself. Turner would be shocked that he, Jarred Maloney, party animal and drunkard, was stone cold sober and watching a woman sleep.

Walking out of the bedroom, he went into the kitchen and cleaned up their mess before turning off all the lights. What the hell was he doing? It was like, well, he was domesticated. Cutting off lights? Cleaning up messes? That wasn't him, yet it felt normal. Jarred looked back toward the bedroom, knowing that he should leave but he couldn't make his feet actually move to the door. He didn't want to leave. He didn't want to go back to his sterile flat and sit in the dark by himself. He didn't want to go out to the club only to think about her the entire time he was there. Jarred knew all he wanted to do really was climb in that bed with Kinsley.

"I'm so fucked," he muttered to himself as he stalked toward the bedroom. She was still there, sleeping as he kicked off his shoes and shed his shirt, stepping out of his trousers, but leaving on his boxer briefs before silently climbing in the bed beside her, careful not to wake her. After pulling the quilt on the end of the bed over the both of them, he looked up at the darkened ceiling and sighed. What was he doing here? What would have happened between them had she not passed out?

14

KINSLEY

Her head felt like it was going to explode. Groaning, Kinsley opened one eye and put her hand over it immediately, the shaft of light splitting her already aching head. What had she done last night? She wasn't one to over imbibe in alcohol, hating the way that she would feel in the morning. Well, like she was this morning.

Rolling over, her hand collided with warm, skin. His sandalwood scent wrapped around her and God, he smelled so good, she couldn't help but inhale. She ran her fingers over the skin and she hummed to herself. She'd pulled someone with amazing muscles and abs.

Slowly her eyes drifted open and she was greeted by Jarred's sleeping face. She jerked back. *Oh shit.*

What the hell had they done last night? Kinsley looked down and blew out a breath when she realized she was still fully clothed. Oh thank heavens. But he was shirtless? Oh hell, had he tucked her in?

Her heart squeezed at the thought. Why was he being so sweet? She was lucky they hadn't slept together.

Sleeping with him would have just complicated things. Not only that, but she would have been wasted and not able to remember a thing. Sleeping with Jarred, that would be something she would want to remember.

Taking a moment, Kinsley looked at Jarred as he slumbered mere inches away from her. He was still gorgeous while he slept, some of the walls he put up to hide his true emotions vanishing. His face was full of sharp lines and angles but they worked for him, his strong jaw dusted with stubble. She loved stubble on a man. His hair was falling across his forehead, her gaze following the lock down the slope of his near perfect nose and equally perfect lips. She had kissed those lips and liked it, a lot. Her eyes followed the slope of his shoulder, seeing the strength of his muscles against his tanned skin. Her hands itched to touch him, to feel the strength for herself, but Kinsley refrained. She didn't want to wake him just yet. With a sigh, she continued her perusal of Jarred while he slept, thinking that not only did he look relaxed, he looked vulnerable, vastly different than the cocky man she was used to seeing. Why was he here if they didn't sleep together? Why had he stayed? Whatever the reason, Kinsley couldn't help but soften to him once again. This was the unexpected turn of events that she could never properly prepare for with Jarred.

His eyes opened suddenly and she cleared her throat. "Um hi."

Surprise flared in his eyes before a curving smile lit up his face. "Hey, good morning."

"I, um," Kinsley started, feeling nearly naked under the quilt despite the fact that she was indeed fully clothed. It was the way he was staring at her, like he could devour her. Was that necessarily such a bad thing? "I apologize for whatever I did last night. I don't normally drink that much."

Jarred rolled over on his back and stretched, giving Kinsley full access to view his spectacular abs in the soft morning light. No man should ever be made to be as gorgeous as Jarred was. She wanted to guide her fingers across his muscles again, feel the strength of him under her fingertips. But she couldn't. Kinsley knew if she did, she wouldn't want to stop. "You didn't do anything," he finally said, throwing back the cover and standing. "Nothing happened."

Kinsley tried not to feel disappointed. Perhaps she had wanted something to happen, to throw caution to the wind and forget herself, even if alcohol had been involved.

"Unless you wanted something to happen."

She looked up sharply, seeing Jarred standing by the bed still, his shirt in his hand. "W-what?" she asked.

"You heard me," he responded, throwing the shirt on the bed, his eyes darkening. "So Kinsley, what do you want?"

"I-I don't know," she blurted out, feeling the rush of need as she saw the outline of his cock in his trousers. He was hard and ready, but was she? Could she handle this between them if they took their relationship, or fake relationship, to the next level?

Jarred climbed back onto the bed and before she realized it, he covered her body with his, only a thin sheet between them. "I think I know what you want," he said in a soft voice. Kinsley gulped as he grasped her shirt and inched it up, until her bra was in full view. "Off," he said, heat in his eyes.

Kinsley complied, her body feeling like rubber as she pulled the shirt over her head, undoing the bra with shaky fingers before throwing it on the floor as well. The look in Jarred's eyes took her breath away as he wasted no time latching onto one of her aching nipples, grasping it gently between his teeth. She moaned, the slight tugging unfurling a knot of heat in her stomach. Her hands went into his hair and instead of pulling him back, she held him there, allowing him to lavish her breast. Her body felt like it was on fire, begging for his touch and she didn't want it to end. When he moved down to her navel, she gripped the edge of the bed sheet tightly, knowing what was coming. And she wanted it.

Jarred quickly divested her of her pants and underwear until Kinsley was naked before him, not feeling ashamed for him to look at her like this. Under his heated gaze, she felt bold and pretty, all of her body imperfections not even coming to mind. This was about she and Jarred and this moment between them.

When his mouth touched her mound, she sighed, the warmth of his lips making her wet with need. His tongue delved until it touched her swollen clit, causing her to nearly buck off of the bed. "Like that?" he said softly against her skin, She moaned, mainly because she couldn't coherently make words form on her tongue and he chuckled, going back to work on her clit. Kinsley concentrated on every flick on his tongue, the warmth, the pressure as he inserted a finger into her before she exploded, the strength of the orgasm surprising her. Her body shook with release before she collapsed on the mattress.

Jarred left the bed, using the bathroom before coming back into the bedroom and sitting on the bed beside her, the smell of her arousal heavy in the air. That had to be the single hottest thing that had happened to her in a while and she couldn't find the words to explain it to him.

Should she offer to do the same? The thought made her slightly excited to do so. To hold the control in her hands, his control, would make her feel powerful. Her mind made up, she sat up quickly, too quickly as the rush of nausea hit her at once. She wasn't going to embarrass herself by throwing up in front of Jarred, not after that.

"You are looking kind of pale," Jarred said as she rubbed her aching temples with her fingers gingerly. "I think you need some food."

The thought of food made her stomach lurch even more. She looked at the clock and swore, throwing back the covers. "I am so late," she muttered. In about ten minutes, her future father-in-law was going to be walking into the office, expecting to see her sitting at her desk.

"Hey," Jarred said, getting Kinsley's attention. "You need food first."

"I have to get to work," she told him, pulling open her dresser drawer in search of some clothes. Not once since she had been working for Mr. Maloney had she ever been late.

Jarred's hand landed on her arm and she looked up, seeing the stormy look on his face. "Listen," he said firmly. "You need food and then we will go see my father together. I'm not taking no for an answer Kinsley."

"Who died and made you in charge?" she countered, feeling even worse that she had to deal with him this morning. It was his fault in the first place that she had drunk all that wine. He made her nervous with just his presence. She couldn't think clearly when he was around.

His hand covered hers, his finger landing on the diamond that Kinsley had gotten quite used to wearing. "This puts me in charge at least temporarily. My father is not going to fire you if you come in late Kinsley, trust me. So, take a nice shower, get dressed, and then we are going to breakfast."

Kinsley opened her mouth to object, but Jarred placed a finger to her lips. "Trust me."

Kinsley

JARRED WAS RIGHT. Kinsley hated to admit it, but a good, solid fry up had done wonders. Now she was sitting in the passenger seat of Jarred's Porsche on their way to meet with his father over these wedding preparations.

"What did we decide last night?" she asked as they pulled into the parking garage. Kinsley wished that she could remember at least something, but her last true memory was of Jarred arriving at her flat and a conversation with him that she couldn't remember the details on. That was it.

"You're going to tell him that every woman wants to plan their own wedding," Jarred answered, pulling the car into a spot and shutting off the engine. "And since he won't let us elope, you are having to change all of the plans of your dream wedding."

"My dream wedding," she echoed, thinking of what that would look like. Unlike other women, she hadn't really thought about her own wedding and certainly hadn't pictured the man beside her as the groom. "Well that should be easy then."

Jarred shot her a look before climbing out of the car, Kinsley following suit. He had been in a mood since they had left her flat this morning, as if he couldn't wait to be rid of her company. It was a far cry from this morning, when she had found him in her bed. Even their breakfast had been awkward, both left to their own thoughts and Kinsley wondered what she had really done last night. Something had passed between them, something that he wasn't telling her.

They walked into the lift and she pressed the button, hoping that she indeed still had a job when this day was over with. What if her boss found out that they had been lying to him the entire time? What would that cause for her? How would Jarred hold up against his father? She should have never agreed to this.

The lift opened to the office floor and Jarred reached down, lacing his fingers with hers.

"W-what are you doing?" she asked softly as they made their way to their destination. His palm was warm against hers and Kinsley found herself wanting to lean against him for some support.

"We're engaged," Jarred said bluntly as they reached the door. "We should play the part. Especially after this morning."

Kinsley flushed and swallowed hard as he pushed open the office door and they walked in, finding her boss seated behind his desk. It was showtime. They needed to talk about this morning. She'd been feeling warm and needy and it shouldn't have happened. They needed to talk about it. But first, they were going to deal with his father.

"Kinsley, Jarred," he said, pointing to the chairs in front of his desk. Kinsley gave him a brief smile as Jarred released her hand and they settled in the chairs. "To what do I owe this pleasure?"

"We are here to talk about the wedding planning," Jarred answered before Kinsley could even open her mouth.

Mr. Maloney raised a brow as he rested his elbows on the desk before him. "Have you? Good. I have the name of the wedding planner right here."

Jarred looked over at Kinsley, who put on a nervous smile. "Actually, sir, I would like to plan my own wedding. I hope you don't mind."

"Call me Harrison, Kinsley," her boss said, looking at his son with a frown on his face. "After all, we are going to be family. Isn't that right Jarred?"

"We are engaged, aren't we?" Jarred ground out. Kinsley fought the urge to roll her eyes against Jarred's response. That wasn't exactly what she would have imagined his father would want to hear.

"We are," she interrupted, giving him a smile. "And I can't wait to become part of this wonderful family, but you are still my boss, Mr. Maloney, and I am afraid I wouldn't feel comfortable calling you by your first name."

His father gave her a warn smile. "That's why you are perfect for my son. You understand respect and decorum. I've been trying to beat it into Jarred for years." Well, that wasn't what she had hoped to hear either. Jarred cleared his throat. Kinsley knew she had to stop this before it became ugly. "I beg to differ sir," she said hastily, laying a hand on Jarred's arm. She could feel the tightness of his muscle under her fingers, anger radiating from every pore. "I adore the way Jarred is. After all, it's what attracted me to him in the first place."

"How is that?" her boss asked, on a laugh. "He has no job, no real drive for the future."

"You asshole," Jarred said under his breath. Kinsley slid her hand down and clasped his tightly, willing him to let her handle this. What his father was saying was wrong.

Just because Jarred didn't have the same drive as her boss did not mean he didn't have a plan. Everyone had a plan. Now whether it was a good plan remained to be seen, but she wasn't going to let him just dog his son like this.

"Jarred is one of the most driven men I know," she answered firmly, looking her boss in the eye. "Did you know he's been sketching his own schematics for concept cars? That he attends all the races? That he has a list of all the driver's stats? He's extremely driven. Just not with what you would see as important. I'm proud to call him my future husband. He has his own dreams." Without a second thought, she leaned over and touched his face with her fingers, forcing him to look at her.

There was shock, confusion, anger in his expression. Though the anger wasn't likely directed at her. Unfortunately, she also saw hurt and embarrassment, which tore at her soul.

His father's words really hurt him and Kinsley wanted nothing more than to soothe that hurt. Her lips somehow found his despite the armrests between them and she attempted to kiss away that look, her heart aching in her chest. Oh hell. First, she'd likely pissed off her boss and she needed this job. Secondly, she'd gone ahead and fallen for Mr. Sex on a Stick. Even though she knew he wasn't anything but trouble. She needed to put the brakes on this somehow. But she couldn't. She was in deep shit.

"Well," his father said as Kinsley pulled away, inwardly shocked by her sudden revelation. "I applaud you then Jarred. I had no idea you had that much interest in the racing company. Seems that you have a great champion in your corner. Not every man is as lucky as you are. If Kinsley believes in you, then I should as well. Maybe when you have some time we can go over your ideas. Meet with Andrew Cordin. He's the EVP of Racing."

Jarred looked down at her, his expression unreadable. "I am a very lucky bastard." Kinsley attempted to smile, her insides churning. She was in love with Jarred Maloney. There was no way anything good was going to come of this now.

15

JARRED

"You have some great ideas Mr. Maloney. Do you mind meeting with our team tomorrow so that we can make some plans?"

Jarred grinned as he looked at the crew chief, James Mills, who ran the Formula One team for Maloney Headquarters, glad that someone thought he had great ideas. His father hadn't been kidding. He'd called Andrew Cordin right away.

He was used to his father being a prick, but in front of Kinsley, it had been humiliating. But what he didn't get was how Kinsley knew all that stuff about him? How could she possibly know?

Either way, she'd blown him away coming to his defense like that. No one had ever crusaded for him before. She'd forced his father into seeing him differently. "Sure," he finally said, realizing the crew chief was still staring at him, waiting for his answer. "I'm open tomorrow."

"Great, just great," James replied. Jarred stood and shook his hand before walking back out to the parking lot where his car was parked. Another car was parked next to his and as he approached, the door opened. Jarred stopped and watched as his mother climbed out of the sleek sedan, smoothing her pencil skirt down as she did so, a tentative smile on her face. "Jarred."

"Mum," he said, wondering how she had found him. "What are you doing here?"

"I was wondering if we could have a spot of tea together," she answered. "There's a nice tea house just down the street."

"I, sure," Jarred answered, thinking that spending time with his mother was the last thing he wanted to do right now. While he and his father didn't get along very well, his relationship with his mother wasn't much better. Pamela Maloney-Gretner had been a model in her former life, hardly ever around when Jarred was growing up. Between his father's business and his mother's profession, Jarred spent more time with his nanny and the servants than any of his family. When Jarred was twelve, his parents divorced and he was thrust back and forth between the two households until he'd been old enough to say no. While his father had never remarried, his mother was married to a banker, a decent fellow who had never pretended to be Jarred's father. That was just fine with him.

Jarred fell in step next to his mother and they walked the block to the tea house, settling just inside the door. After ordering their tea, Jarred looked at his mother. "So, why the parental concern all of a sudden?"

"Oh Jarred," she sighed, her red-tipped fingernails drumming on the table. "Can't I just want to see my son?"

"No," Jarred answered, crossing his arms over his chest. "You can't."

"Fine," she frowned as their tea arrived. "I hear that you are engaged to be married, *again*."

Jarred chose to ignore the way she said the last word. After being around Kinsley, he wished his engagement to Susan had never occurred. Kinsley was so much more than Susan had ever been to him and the display that she had shown this morning only confirmed what he already knew. Of all the women he could have chosen for this task, Kinsley was the only one that could make it work. Now he was concerned that she was going to take more than just his money. Like his heart. "I am."

"I also hear that your father has cut you off until you do," she continued, looking at him curiously. "So I find that very odd that you have jumped right into a relationship."

"The engagement is real Mother," he said with a sigh. "Kinsley is my fiancée."

"She's *not* Susan," she countered, taking a sip of her coffee. "I don't know why you broke it off with Susan. She is such a lovely girl. Plus, she would be good for your image Jarred. Just think of the social implications. Susan could have elevated your status to some of the best names in London."

Jarred rubbed a hand over his face, knowing this was a mistake. Society and their opinions was all that his mother cared about. The plastic surgery, the rich husband, the expensive clothes, they were all his mother thought about. "What if I'm in love? Doesn't that matter at all?"

His mother laughed, waving a hand at him. "Oh Jarred. That is the most ridiculous thing I have ever heard. Love? Love doesn't exist. Mutual respect, yes, but love, now that's rich coming from you."

Jarred's eyes narrowed. "What does that mean?"

She smiled. "Nothing darling, but you are your father's son. All that Harrison Maloney cared about and still cares about is that business of his and the money that he is raking in. Do you know the day we got married he went back to work? No honeymoon, no nothing. It was like I never existed." His mother then leaned forward, her massive diamond rings twinkling in the morning light. "Love is for those who have nothing else in their life. Love makes you weak, Jarred, and you would be best served to remember that."

Jarred heard his mother's words, but he wasn't so sure that they were right. Kinsley wasn't making him weak. After today, he felt like he was someone else in her eyes, someone that gave a damn. Her words were part of the reason he'd come on to the meeting at the garage, wanting to prove her right and his father wrong. Today had proven what he knew all along: he was damn near in love with Kinsley. Somehow, in some fashion, she had wormed her way into his heart and he was fucking scared to death at the thought of loving her, disappointing her, not being the man she deserved.

"Are you not in love with Preston?" Jarred decided to ask, thinking of the man that his mother was currently settled down with.

A look passed over his mother's face before she shook her head, looking flustered all of a sudden. "Preston and I have mutual respect for each other. I-I care for Preston, but I'll never love again. Your father killed that feeling for me years ago." She reached across the table and touched his hand briefly, her expression softening just a bit. "I have always hoped the best for you Jarred and if this woman is someone you can live with, then I can't change your mind, but be smart about this. Don't let this woman in. Nothing good ever comes out of falling in love. I am living proof of that."

Jarred withdrew from her touch, his mind in a whirlwind of thoughts and feelings that he still had to sort out. Kinsley was someone very special to him, there wasn't a doubt in his mind about that. But did he want to take their relationship to the next level? What would he have felt if they had slept together last night? Would he be questioning his feelings for her now?

Without saying a word to his mother, Jarred threw some bills on the table and walked away, reaching into his pocket for his cell phone. He knew what he needed to do. Why hadn't he thought of this before?

Jarred

"So, where are we going?" Kinsley asked as Jarred threw the car into drive and started down the road. The sun was setting on the horizon, the disastrous day almost over with. After meeting with his mother, Jarred had fired off two text messages: one to Kinsley inviting her out tonight and one to Turner, telling him to find a damn date so they could double date tonight. He needed Turner to meet Kinsley and see if she was the real deal. Turner wouldn't hold back and Jarred trusted that his friend would voice his opinion or make Jarred crazy— which he didn't know. The woman beside him was making him bloody crazy enough.

"We are going out. I already told you," he finally answered. "With a friend of mine."

Kinsley didn't say anything immediately as Jarred turned down a street, his jaw clenched tightly. He was on edge, concerned about his growing feelings for Kinsley and the fact that this farce of an engagement was no longer just a farce. At least not for him. "You'll like Turner," he added. "He's not a bad fellow."

"Jarred," she said softly, looking over at him with concern on her face. "Why are you doing this? Is this about this morning? We should probably talk about—"

Christ, he could still taste her, sweet and spicy. Jarred cleared his throat, wishing he had an answer to just fire back at her. Hell, he wasn't sure why he was going to these lengths. So, he went with what he considered as the truth. "I want to spend time with you. Is that a crime?"

She didn't say anything as he pulled into the parking lot and shut off the engine, climbing out before he lost his nerve and took her home. He rounded the back of the car as Kinsley was climbing out, pinning her against the car with his body before she could take a step forward. She looked up at him, her eyes wide with surprise as he reached out, cupping her cheek with his hand. "I'm sorry," he said roughly. "I shouldn't be an ass." The day's events, the meetings with his parents, still had him on edge and he was taking it out on the one person that had stood up for him today.

She wet her lips, giving him a small smile. "Well your day didn't start out very well."

"Actually, it started freaking fantastic." He dropped his forehead to hers. "I could taste you all day, spicy on my tongue," he said softly, his thumb stroking her soft cheek. "Thank you for what you said to my father this morning." God, he wanted to kiss her again so badly. She had done something that no one else had ever done for him, not even Susan.

"It's the truth," she answered. "Why can't you see that?"

Surprised, Jarred looked at her. "What?" he asked, a sudden pain in his chest appearing out of nowhere.

Kinsley shrugged. "I mean, you can be that person Jarred. I believe you already are, to tell you the truth, but you just have to show it."

Shaken, Jarred stepped back, releasing her so that she wouldn't see the way her words had affected him. She had so much faith in him and it was frightening. "How did you know about the cars and the sketches?"

"Jarred." Her voice shook. "I saw them in your flat that first night we met. They were really good."

Jarred turned to see Turner approaching, a petite redhead with glasses on his arm. "Bugger off. I didn't think you were ever going to get here," Turner said as he reached them. "Ms. Wells. It's a pleasure."

"Kinsley, please," Kinsley replied, sticking out her hand. "You must be Turner."

"This is Mary," Turner said, a grin on his face as he introduced his date, who was looking at them both curiously. "We, ah, work together."

"I'm the broad that keeps him in check," Mary supplied, laughing as she shook both of their hands. "Mary Blisser. Nice to meet you both."c Jarred liked her immediately. Turner looked so fucking happy that Jarred felt that his friend was going to burst open at any moment. Did he look that way around Kinsley? Bloody hell.

"Well, shall we get our bowl on then?" Turner was saying, referring to the bowling alley behind them. Jarred's plan wasn't his normal nightly fare but something fun, that he hadn't done in quite a while.

"I love bowling," Kinsley answered, looking up at Jarred. He took in her smiling expression and wanted to kiss the hell out of her right then and there. Screw Turner. Susan had never looked at him like that. She would have wrinkled her nose, complained about everything in bloody London if he'd dragged her to something like this. Jarred forced a tight smile, reaching down to grab her hand instead. He needed to touch her, to assure himself that this was very real and not just some weird dream. "Well, let's not wait any longer then."

16

KINSLEY

She was having fun. The realization hit her as she threw the ball down the lane, watching as it knocked down a few pins before turning around to give Jarred a high five. Jarred had loosened up as well, her earlier concerns that something was really wrong now in the back of her mind. He grabbed her around the waist and spun her around, making her laugh aloud. She liked this Jarred.

"Stop," she said, lightly hitting his shoulder so that he would put her down. He grinned and kissed her forehead before doing so, grabbing his ball to set up for his turn. Kinsley had noted that tonight he'd been more touchy feely than ever, like he was really wanting to do it. After all, she was sure that Turner knew the truth about their arrangement. She sat down next to Turner, finding Jarred's friend very likeable. He was the complete opposite of

Jarred and Kinsley was really surprised that they were friends.

"So you think he will get another gutter ball?" Turner said as they watched Jarred wait for the lane to be cleared of pins. "Jarred is horrid at bowling."

"It shows," she giggled, looking up at Jarred's score. It was truly dreadful.

"You know, I think he loves you," Turner said softly as Jarred started his approach to the lane. "You make him happy."

Kinsley's throat seemed to close up then, unable to find the words to refute that claim. She wanted to be the one to make him happy. Jarred deserved happiness. "I—I," she started. Turner chuckled, laying a hand on her arm briefly.

"Don't worry, he doesn't know it yet, but he will. Just … He's my best mate, the only person I trust in this miserable world. Please don't hurt him."

"I won't," Kinsley said softly, watching as Jarred rolled the ball down the lane before walking back toward them, a frown on his handsome face. She didn't want to hurt him. Jarred had been hurt enough in his life. She wanted to be that person that made it all better for him.

"Hey you got two pins," Turner announced as Mary came up to stand beside his chair. "That's got to be a record."

"Bugger off," Jarred muttered, running a hand through his hair. "I never liked this damn game anyway."

"You only don't like it because you are horrid at it," Turner laughed, looking at Kinsley. "Maybe you should teach him a thing or two. You're pretty good at this bowling thing."

Kinsley blushed as she looked up at the scores, seeing that she was in the lead. She and Rachel had bowled as kids, spending Friday nights wasting their time in a place just like this.

"As long as they're private lessons," Jarred announced, giving her a wink. "Then I don't mind."

Private. Kinsley wanted to be with him privately, again. Feeling his tongue on her heated folds. She wanted to explore his body, make him grin and laugh more and lose those shadows in his eyes. Never in her life had she wanted anyone as much as she wanted Jarred right now. The thought was terrifying.

They finished the game and turned in their equipment, walking out into the crisp night air. Kinsley walked close to Jarred, her arm brushing against his as they made their way to the car. "Let's go to the club," Mary announced, her arm around Turner's waist. "I want to dance."

"I want to sleep," Turner muttered, looking at them. "Well? What do you think? Shall we hit the club?"

"I'm actually quite tired," Kinsley answered. "It's been a long day."

"I'm beat as well," Jarred said. Turner looked at them both and slowly nodded, though his expression wasn't very believing of either of their excuses. "Well then, we shall say good night then," he said.

They said their good-byes and Kinsley climbed in the car, her heart pounding in her chest. She wasn't the least bit tired, but there was something else she wanted, something that was just now climbing in the car himself. She just had to figure out a way to ask for it.

Jarred slid behind the steering wheel and it wasn't long before they were on the road, heading toward her side of town. "So," he said, his hands gripping the wheel. "Is there anything else you want to do tonight? It's still early."

Kinsley swallowed. Should she tell him what she really wanted to do? What would he say? Would he want to have sex with her? "I, um," she started, her tongue tripping over her words. "I want to go home."

He nodded. "I'm sure you haven't recovered from your, uh, wine last night either."

"I want us to go home," Kinsley blurted out, her voice sounding small in the vehicle. Jarred pulled up to a red traffic light and looked over at her, his eyes heated.

"What did you say?" he asked.

"I want *us* to go home," she said again, her voice louder this time. "Together."

He worked his jaw for a moment. "Are you sure?" he finally asked, his voice low.

She nodded and he took off, covering the last few blocks in what seemed like seconds. Now nervous, Kinsley didn't look at him, instead focusing on the scenery out of the window. She was taking a giant leap by sleeping with Jarred. She had already lost her heart to him and rapidly losing the rest of herself to her fake fiancé as well. Now all that remained was to find out what Jarred was feeling or not feeling about her. If Turner's words were true, Kinsley wasn't making a mistake in this decision.

Jarred parked the car on the street and they both climbed out, Kinsley taking Jarred's hand in a bold move as they approached her building. He wrapped his hand around hers tightly, giving her a smile. "No wine tonight?"

She laughed, some of the tension easing. "No, no wine tonight. Or beer. Or liquor."

"Okay, I got the point," he said as they walked into the lift, Kinsley pressing the button for her floor. As soon as the doors closed, Jarred turned her in his arms, trapping her against the wall and his body. Kinsley's breath left her lungs as she looked up at Jarred, her pulse drumming just under her skin. He leaned down and brushed a hair from her shoulder, the smell of his cologne filling her senses.

"Are you sure about this?" he asked softly, his breath on her cheek.

"I—I am," she breathed as he dropped a kiss on her cheek. She was more than ready.

The lift doors opened and Jarred stepped back. Kinsley took the moment to catch her breath as they walked down the hall together, close enough to touch. Her fingers fumbled with her keys but she managed to get the door unlocked, stepping into the dark interior of her flat. Jarred shut the door and grabbed her from behind, pulling her roughly against him. She could feel his erection on her ass, the way his hands gripped her waist tightly as if she was going to bolt at any second. Her weak knees wouldn't allow it.

He sighed, his lips nibbling at her neck as they stood there in the hall, the darkness all around them. "No lights," Jarred whispered. "No clothes. Just you and me."

"Yes," Kinsley said softly. This wasn't wrong. Jesus, she wanted this. They had tiptoed around this intense heat between the two of them and it was time to abate this fire. She turned around in his arms and grasped the edge of his shirt, helping pull it over his head before her hands landed on his warm skin, feeling his strength under her fingers. Lazily, she ran her hands over his chest, touching the planes of his muscles down to his rock hard abs, the ridges both soft and hard under her fingers.

When she brushed his belt, Jarred groaned. "You're killing me Kinsley."

"We can't have that," she whispered, undoing his belt with trembling fingers until his jeans were around his ankles and he was stepping out of them. Her hand brushed against his cock and she gasped. Jarred reached down with a firm hand and guided her hand to him again. "Please touch me," he said, his voice coming out in a hoarse whisper.

She wrapped her fingers around the length of him, gripping tightly. A low moan escaped from his lips as she explored him in the dark, unable to see but she could feel the hard length of him, her own body burning up, melting.

"You have too many clothes on," Jarred murmured, his voice strained as he reached for her shirt, pulling it over her head. She released him with reluctance to get her shirt off, and he was already working on her jeans as she slid off her bra. When she was naked before him, he pulled her to him, crushing her body against his hard planes, engaging her in a hot kiss, ravaging her mouth with his.

Kinsley clung to him, her thoughts scattering. This was what she wanted, to be close to Jarred like this. She wanted him to make her feel. She wanted to be desired.

He backed her up against the wall, rattling the table in the foyer in the process. "Bed," Jarred mumbled against her neck, his teeth nipping at the sensitive skin there. "Now."

She nodded as he bodily moved them to her bedroom, falling on the bed before he covered her body with his. She could feel the stiff length of him at her center, her body arching against him, urging him on.

She was beyond ready for him. Jarred pulled away, one of his hands smoothing her hair off of her head. In the dim light of the room, Kinsley could see the heated expression on his face, the need that she felt in her body. "Slow," he said, his hand sliding down her chest to cup her breast. "We are taking it slow."

"No," she said, grabbing at his shoulders.

He chuckled, tweaking her nipple between his fingers. "Persistent, are we?"

"Desperate," she gasped as his hand slipped lower, caressing her stomach before dipping lower, his finger finding her wet slit. Kinsley closed her eyes and gave herself up to his touch.

Feeling the pressure build with each swipe of his finger. This was far beyond their first encounter. He continued to kiss her, his tongue seeking hers. With a low curse, he rolled away, reaching for his jeans.

In the darkness she could hear something ripping and then he was pack, his weight pressing her thighs open again. They were going to be on another level after this.

Stroke by stroke, his fingers took her higher. Took her to the edge of bliss and back again. But then he swiped over her clit with his thumb.

When the orgasm hit her, he growled and pushed into her, filling her deep. She arched against the weight of him, her body quivering around him as he stayed there, allowing her to adjust to the feel of him. "You're so fucking wet," Jarred whispered, leaning down to brush his lips over hers. She returned his kiss, her legs wrapping around him and pulling him deeper. "I need you," she panted.

"You've got me," he answered, moving over her. Kinsley kept her eyes opened, marveling in the concentration on his face, the way his jaw was clenched tightly as he moved in and out slowly. She reached up and cupped his cheek, forcing him to look at her. The emotions in his eyes, they were emotions she hadn't anticipated on seeing.

Another orgasm hit her body and her hand started to slip before he grasped it lightly, bringing it back up to his face. Her heart lurched in her chest as he pumped in and out of her, his movements becoming frenzied. "Yes," she urged him on, raising her body to meet his thrusts. "Yes."

He let out a groan before stiffening, and holding himself over her before his body collapsed on hers. Kinsley could feel the rapid beating of his heart against her own chest, mimicking her own pulse. It was hard to even believe what had just happened, though she knew this changed things, a lot of things.

17

JARRED

Jarred collapsed on his back, feeling weightless. What had just passed between them, it was hard to describe but he wanted to fucking do it again. And again. Rolling over, he found Kinsley lying there, her even breathing nothing compared to the jumbled up thoughts in his mind about where this took them. He had no idea where this took them, only that he wanted to do it again. "Hey," he finally said, pushing himself up on one elbow.

She turned and gave him a sleepy smile. "Hey."

"So, I was thinking," he continued, his finger reaching out to touch her shoulder lightly. She shivered under his touch and Jarred was instantly hard, wondering what she would say if he decided to go again. "That I could sleep for a damn week."

She blushed. "Me too." He reached over and pulled her against him until his body was curled around her warm one, his arms encircling her body gently. She sighed and Jarred grinned, trying to think of the last time he'd wanted to do this cuddling shit with a woman.

Even though he could bury himself between her thighs once more, Jarred was currently happy just doing this as well, hearing her little sighs and feeling her wiggle against him as she fought to get comfortable. She was killing him in more ways than one. He felt her body relax against his and sighed inwardly himself, wondering at what point in his life he'd turned into the guy who was content to cuddle with a woman. No, not just any woman but Kinsley. Only Kinsley.

He shifted slightly and she rolled toward him, murmuring something intelligible before curling up against him once more, a smile on her face. Yeah, this was a good thing. Jarred knew that now. What if this was real? What if he could have every night with Kinsley like this one? Did he want to do this?

Looking at her beautiful face, Jarred felt a tug in his chest suspiciously close to his heart. Hell yeah he wanted to.

Jarred

THE NEXT MORNING Jarred entered the Formula One headquarters, whistling as he walked to the conference room. He felt fucking great after his night with Kinsley, leaving this morning before she woke up and the awkward morning could occur. It had been extremely hard leaving her in that bed, naked, but it had been the right thing to do. She needed to get used to the fact that he wasn't going anywhere now and a few hours to herself should allow for that. But he couldn't wait to see her again.

Now he was heading to his 'job,' the one thing that had held his interest for longer than two seconds of his life. After Kinsley had gone to bat for him in front of his father, the partnership with Andrew Cordin was really taking off.

They guy seemed genuinely interested in what Jarred had to say and today they were working on a concept for the cars for the new racing season, a thought he'd read up on that seemed to be working in other parts of the world. It was a good feeling knowing that someone thought he was worth the stuff that was coming out of his mouth, that they believed he knew what he was talking about. This racing team was the reason he got up in the morning now, well, that and Kinsley. "I'm fucked," he muttered to himself with a grin, not caring anymore. What he had going on was a good problem to have.

"Jarred," Andrew said as he entered the conference room, a grin on his own face. "Glad to see you. You ready to get started?"

"Yeah," Jarred said as he sat in one of the chairs, a good feeling in his body. "I am."

After a few hours with Andrew, Jarred made some plans and went to his flat for a shower and change, intending to catch Kinsley off guard this evening. It was around six when he finally made it over to headquarters, feeling like a million bucks and anxious to see Kinsley.

He had thought about her all day, surprised how many times she had crossed his mind. If this was what he thought it was, he was truly fucking in love with Kinsley Wells. The thought didn't scare him like it should have. She had been the one person that had stood up for him, saw him as the guy that he had tried to be but wasn't given much of a chance to do so. She had given him that chance and he was going to spend the rest of his life paying her back for it.

As the lift doors opened to his father's office floor, Jarred spied her sitting alone at her desk, most of the lights off except the one directly over her. There was no noise on the floor, and there was dead silence with the exception of the key strokes she was making on her computer. She looked up and their eyes met, hers widening as she watched him approach. "J-Jarred," she said, standing abruptly. "What are you doing here?"

"Coming for you," he said, taking in her dress and heels, her hair up in a prim knot. She looked nothing like the woman he'd shagged last night and it was fucking driving him crazy. His cock strained against his pants and he swallowed hard, feeling the need to touch her in any way.

She gave him a slight smile, crossing her arms over her chest. "For me? Why?"

"Well," he said, crossing his own arms over his chest to mimic her stance. "I figured I needed to make up for bailing on you this morning before we could go another round."

She blushed then, clearly remembering just what they'd done before he had to leave in the morning. Hell, he couldn't forget it himself.

"It's fine. I mean it's good."

"No it's not," he said, dropping his arms and closing the gap between them until the desk was the only thing between them. "Let me take you to dinner."

She tucked a stray hair behind her ear, a soft smile on her face. "That's, uh, very nice of you Jarred."

There wasn't anything *nice* about his thoughts right now, and it was her fault. He couldn't think of anything but her and what he would like to do to her. And her scent … and her soft skin. And the way she said his name on a breathy sigh.

Stepping around the desk, he tugged her against him, her soft body melting against his rock hard one. "I'm not a nice guy," he said softly, leaning down to brush his lips against her soft cheek. Her perfume tantalized him, drawing him in and Jarred didn't know why he suddenly liked the smell of vanilla but on Kinsley, he liked everything.

"Yes you are," she said, her breath coming out on a rush. "I've seen it."

Jarred grinned then, bringing his hand up to brush over the cheek he'd just kissed. "You'll ruin my reputation. Shall I show you how *bad* I can be?"

"W-what?" she stammered.

Jarred's other hand slid up her arm and down her back, gripping her ass lightly until she gasped in surprise, a glimmer of heat flaring in her eyes. "Are we alone Ms. Wells?"

She jerked her head up and down and Jarred's grin grew wider, his hand finding the hem of her dress and inching it up, slowly. "Well then, I have something to show you."

18

KINSLEY

All Kinsley's breath left her body as she felt Jarred's hand caress her bare hip, and she saw the flare of passion in his own eyes as he realized she wasn't wearing any knickers. She didn't know what made her do that this morning, but as she had slipped on the dress, a small piece of her wanted to do something naughty. After last night, she felt like a different woman.

"I have to tell you, I like the new style," he murmured, his fingers brushing over her mound. She shivered lightly, the spiral of heat unfurling in her belly. "Did you do that for me Kinsley?"

"Y-yes." Kinsley nodded, unable to speak as his fingers found what they were looking for. His middle finger slid over her clit gently and she gasped. When his finger dipped into her heated center, she couldn't help a moan. The look on his face was fierce, sweat beading on his forehead as he stroked her. His narrow eyed gaze completely focused on her as he added another finger. When her breath hitched and her core tightened around him, his lids lowered down and he cursed low. "Fuck, Kinsley." As he drove her mad, her hands gripped the edge of the desk tightly.

"Oh." He whispered. "I suppose I should tell you how happy that makes me. Or maybe I should show you instead?"

She arched her back into his caress. "B-Both."

He grinned. "I know you like it when I slide a finger inside you. Want to know how I can tell?"

"How?"

"Because of that little sound you make at the back of your throat. I love that sound." He slid another one inside her, curling them and gently stroking over her G-spot

Her knees buckled. "Oh, God." Another moan escaped her lips.

"God, I love that sound." He grinned and rubbed again. Kinsley had no choice but to hold on tight to his shoulders as he slid his fingers inside of her.

She dug her nails into his shoulders as her inner walls clung to his fingers. Kinsley cried out his name, her soft cries captured when he kissed her.

Jarred tore his lips from hers. "Do you have any idea how much I love feeling you clamp around my fingers?"

"Oh, God. Please—"

He pulled another orgasm from her with another gentle stroke of his middle and index fingers. "Kinsley, I need to be inside you." He nuzzled her neck as he spoke. "All day I've been distracted thinking about you how you feel, how you taste. Your laugh, everything."

Kinsley licked her lips and reached for him. She kept her eyes on his as she pulled his belt free from its buckle. His cock free, her core pulsed again. How could she want him again?

Jarred gripped her waist and turned her around, bending her over the desk. He shoved the fabric of her dress up over her hips and Kinsley held her breath, waiting for him to claim her.

But his touch was soft at first. Caressing, instead of claiming, and he was driving her mad. But that was probably all part of his nefar—Oh hell. He slid his fingers into her again and she moaned low. "Please Jarred, I need you."

"Shh, don't worry. I know what you need. I'm just trying to make you feel good."

Kinsley moaned low. "Jarred Please."

"I'm not letting you go, you know that. You are so bloody sexy like this." With a murmured curse, he sank deep.

Holy hell he was so big. As always the fit was snug, but deliciously so. She could

feel every pulse of his length. And she relished the way his hands tightened on her hips.

"Fuck, Kinsley. I…can't…Jesus…so tight."

She'd never felt like this in her life. Like she could snap in half with wanting someone. Jarred withdrew gently, inch by inch, and Kinsley moaned low. "Faster."

But Jarred kept making love to her slowly. Sinking in deep, filling her, owning her, then sliding out. Kinsley couldn't take the slow torture any more and she canted her hips back toward him. That did the trick. He slid an arm around her waist, then slid down to her clit.

Gently stroking her, he leaned forward and nipped her shoulder. "Okay, sweetheart, I'll give you what you want."

And did he ever. The pace increased as if someone had snapped a rubber band inside him. His grip was tight as he lost control and he took her deep. His fingers worked their magic over her clit and Kinsley would swear she saw stars. Holy hell. But it was what he did next that had her souring before she even knew what happened.

As he teased her with tight circles on her slit followed by lazy stroking, bringing her to the edge and back, with his other hand he released her hip, switching his hold to her ass. It was only when his thumb grazed over her pucker that she went perfectly still.

Jarred stopped moving as he filled her. "You okay?"

"Jarred, what—"

"Shh. How does it feel?"

His fingers gently pressed against her clit even as he stroked his thumb just over were their bodies were joined, before tracing over her pucker. "I—" Oh God. The sensation was different. Foreign, but good. And *naughty*. "Good. It feels good."

"Then that's all you need to worry about." He pulled back again, but this time when he sank deep, his thumb slid past the pucker of her ass. With his thumb and forefinger, he gently pinched her clit and Kinsley was soaring. The sensations were too much, her head was spinning and her body was on fire.

Even though her body was shaking, he kept making love to her, sinking deep, his name a constant whisper on his lips. His thumb kept pace with the hard length of him and before she knew it, she was coming again.

Finally, when she thought she couldn't take it anymore, Jarred stiffened, pouring himself into her, his teeth nipping at her nape.

Kinsley's breathing was harsh in her own ears as she started to float down to earth. What had they just done … on her desk no less? In her workplace? Bloody hell, she had really lost it. Her need to be close to Jarred again had made her lose all rational thought and though she should be extremely embarrassed and ashamed, she wasn't. This just felt right. Well, maybe not on the desk but this thing with Jarred, it felt right.

"Well, did I show you?" he chuckled as he eased out of her.

Kinsley straightened and adjusted her dress, a smile curving on her lips as she turned to face him. Damn him, he looked no different than he had when he walked in, a gorgeous, dangerous man who had stolen her heart. She loved him. The thought was terrifying still, but the feeling, it was stronger than before. Without a word, she reached up and kissed him on the lips. "You showed me all right. Now, you owe me dinner."

Jarred grinned and held out his arm. "Your wish is my command."

Kinsley grinned as well, looking back at her desk hopelessly. It didn't look like she had just shagged there, but every time she would come in to work now, she would picture herself facedown as Jarred shagged her from behind. As he used his thumb on hidden, forbidden places. She'd lost it. And it was too late to go back now.

Jarred tugged on her arm and she followed him to the lift, leaning into his body just to feel his warmth around her again. He released her arm as they entered the lift, sliding his arm around her waist and pulling her closer. "You are so naughty," he said against her ear.

Kinsley giggled, mainly because she didn't know what else to do, her fingers trailing down his chest. This was craziness, major craziness.

Jarred led her out of the lift and to his car, helping her climb in before shutting the door. Kinsley leaned against the headrest, a stupid smile on her face. She was happy. *He* was making her happy. There was no faking what was going on right now.

Jarred climbed in and started the engine, giving her a grin as he backed the car up. He looked happy. Was he happy? She couldn't help but wonder what was going through his mind at this moment. Was she more than just a good shag? She wanted to spend every waking moment with him now, exploring the real Jarred Maloney. But something told Kinsley she had barely scratched the surface.

But did he want to do the same? Did he see her as something more? She sure hoped so. "Um Jarred?" she started as he pulled out onto the street.

"Yeah?" he asked, his eyes on the road.

"See my friend, my cousin, you met her that one night, Rachel. She's getting married in two days," she started, fidgeting with the sleeve of her dress. "I was wondering if you would like to be my date, you know for the rehearsal dinner and the wedding?"

He slowed the car to a stop at the traffic light and looked over at her, giving her a grin that lit up his entire face. Kinsley's breath caught as she took in the sight. Yes, she was most definitely in love with this man. "I'd love to," he said softly. "There's nothing else I would rather do."

Kinsley returned his smile with one of her own, her heart full with happiness. This was going to work out, she just knew it.

Kinsley

THE NEXT NIGHT, Kinsley stood next to the other bridesmaids as she watched Rachel giggle through her vows, looking utterly ridiculous with the bows in her hair but feeling nothing but love and happiness for her friend.

Jamison's smile could not get any bigger as he grasped Rachel's hand and Kinsley could feel the love radiating off of the two as they practiced for the biggest day of their life, their wedding day that would happen against a stunning backdrop of white roses. The weather was already starting to shape up perfectly for an outdoor wedding, which was what Kinsley was hoping for. Nothing should get in the way of her best friend getting married.

Looking over, she caught Jarred's eye as he sat amongst the empty pews waiting for her so they could go to the wedding rehearsal dinner. He looked devastatingly handsome in his black suit, her heart pounding against her chest just by looking at him. This morning had been the first time she had woken to find him in her bed. Almost like he was part of her life.

He *was* part of her life and she didn't want him to leave. Their initial reason of getting together wasn't even in play anymore. She wanted Jarred, all of him. He winked at her and she gave him a saucy smile. After the wedding tomorrow she would tell him how she felt and hope that he felt the same way. Kinsley was tired of hiding behind this farce, knowing that she was no longer pretending but living in these tender feelings. It was time to put it all out on the line and hope that it was going to have a good ending.

19

JARRED

He loved her. The thought hit him more than once as they listened to the toasts to the happy couple, everyone clearly excited about the upcoming nuptials. He glanced over to see the tears in Kinsley's eyes as she gripped his hand. This was every woman's dream. It wasn't hard to see that Rachel and Jamison loved each other. The truth was written on their faces.

Jarred had never seen those looks until he met Kinsley and now the entire fucking world was different. Now when he woke up in the mornings, she was the first thing on his mind. It wasn't such a bad feeling. Now his life had shifted focus and Kinsley was the center of it. He wanted to prove to her that he was the guy she had always looked for, the guy she deserved. He wanted to show her that he was a good guy. More than that, he wanted to give her what they were witnessing tonight. He wanted to see that shining happiness when she looked at him, feel the excitement of making her his wife. That's what he wanted. Never had Jarred ever wanted anything so much before. He would go to the ends of the earth to make her happy.

"Don't they look so happy?" she whispered as they watched Jamison serenade his bride-to-be with a song that was horribly off key. But the bride-to-be was crying and everyone else was sighing, so Jarred guessed it didn't matter that the groom clearly didn't know how to sing.

Bringing their joined hands up to his lips, Jarred kissed the back of her hand, the ring he'd given her in the beginning catching his eye. That ring stood for a farce of a relationship but now, now they had something real and precious. He wanted to show her that he meant business now and a new ring, with a proper proposal, would fix that. After the wedding he would tell her how he felt and propose for real this time, hoping that he would see the love in her eyes as he did so. If not, well there wasn't enough alcohol in all of England to erase the pain that he would feel.

They rode home together later, Kinsley talking nonstop about the wedding tomorrow, telling him of her cousin's worries and fears. "I don't know why she's so worried," she said as he drove them down the street. "I mean, she's marrying a man that can't live without her. Even if the bottom falls out of the sky, nothing is going to dim that."

"He loves her," Jarred said, gripping the steering wheel tightly. "Nothing will get in the way of him making her his wife. He will go to the ends of the earth to make her smile." Kinsley said nothing and Jarred dared not to look at her. He knew his words weren't about just Jamison and Rachel; they were about him and Kinsley. He would go to the ends of the earth for her just to see her smile. He had to have her and no one else would ever compare. Jarred had only thought he'd loved Susan. What he had with Kinsley, it was a feeling he couldn't describe and he never wanted to live without it.

Jarred

THE NEXT DAY, he walked down Brook Street towards Oxford Street after a meeting at Claridge's. His meeting with Adam had gone well. The concept he'd dreamed up was coming along nicely and the board executives that had visited this morning had also enjoyed the thought process. If all went well, the new cars would be debuting this time next year and making his father and the company a great deal of money.

He wanted to celebrate with Kinsley, but it would have to wait as the wedding of her cousin was later on today and he had an obligation to attend. No, obligation wasn't the right word. An obligation meant he'd hate every fucking minute of it but the thought of seeing Kinsley in her bridesmaid gown, of dancing with her until the wee hours of the morning and right before they fell into bed together, of telling her how he felt, was almost too much to take in. It was going to be an epic night and he couldn't wait for the hours to tick by so he could see her again.

She was currently with the bride, doing all of that pre-wedding shit women liked to do. Jarred hadn't seen her since he'd dropped her off at her cousin's parents' house, kissing her long and hard on their doorstep. The bride had asked her to spend the night with her one last time before she became a married woman and Jarred had reluctantly gone to his own flat, finding it empty and lonely since Kinsley wasn't there with him. It had been a long, sleepless night and he was ready to start the next phase of his life, with her by his side. He just had to get through the next few hours.

Walking down another block, Jarred spied the jewelry store up ahead, his mind set on getting Kinsley another ring, one that would symbolize his love this time. She deserved a token of his affection and not one that had been built upon a lie.

"Jarred!"

Turning around, he saw Susan hurrying toward him, dark sunglasses on her face. She was dressed impeccably, as if the thought of having one single hair out of place disgusted her. Jarred himself much preferred Kinsley's bedhead than to his ex, but he stood on the sidewalk anyway, his hands in his pockets. He could be civil. After all, they had both found love in different places. "Susan."

"Oh Jarred," she said, pushing the sunglasses back to reveal red-rimmed eyes. "I was having tea at Claridge's when I saw you. I don't know what to do. "

Surprised by her outburst, he watched as her eyes filled up with tears. He had never seen her so distraught before. "What's wrong?" he asked politely, wishing that he hadn't stopped now.

She sniffed, pulling out a handkerchief to dab at her eyes. "It's Baron. He's cheating on me. I know he is."

Feeling awkward, Jarred wanted to tell her that she had gotten herself into this mess. He couldn't help that her husband was cheating. Hell, the entire social scene knew that Baron was never the type to be faithful and marriage wasn't going to change that. But that wasn't *his* problem, not anymore. "Listen," he said, wanting to give her some kind of advice at least. "Don't stay if you think this isn't going to work. Life's too fucking short to settle for anything less than what you deserve."

Her eyes widened. "Who are you and what have you done with Jarred Maloney?"

"I'm just a different person now," he shrugged. He wasn't about to share with her what was making him different now, even if it was apparent. "Just think about what I said."

Susan closed her mouth, a slight smile appearing on her lips. "And to think, I could be that lucky girl."

"You were that lucky girl," he reminded her gently. "Goodbye Susan."

Before he realized what was happening, Susan was pressing her lips to his, the overpowering smell of her perfume making his stomach turn. He pushed her away, wiping at his mouth as he walked away angrily. She had her chance and now his future was with Kinsley. It couldn't come soon enough.

20

KINSLEY

Kinsley fluffed out the skirt of the dress and then stood back, tears coming to her eyes as she looked at Rachel all decked out for the first time. "You look beautiful," she breathed as her cousin looked at her reflection in the mirror.

Rachel turned around and Kinsley saw that there were tears in her eyes as well, smoothing down the tulle skirt. "I just, I can't believe that this day is finally here. I feel like it has been a long time coming but now that it's here, I just don't know what to do."

Kinsley smiled, wiping at the tears hastily so that they wouldn't ruin her carefully applied makeup. "You're going to walk down that aisle and say your vows. That's what you are going to do."

Rachel gave her a teary smile and turned back to the mirror. "Yes, that's what I am going to do."

Kinsley couldn't help but feel happiness for Rachel and Jamison, knowing that what Rachel had said was true. They had waited a good while to make this official, but today they would become husband and wife. The feeling had to be amazing in itself. For a split second, she tried to picture herself in Rachel's shoes, walking down the aisle to find Jarred at the end of it, waiting for them to become one in the eyes of their friends and family, her heart racing at the fact that it could happen and not in some kind of false way in order to get Jarred's trust fund and her flat. It was no longer about either of those things, or at least she liked to hope that it wasn't. For her, it was about the love she felt for him, the way he made her happy. Life seemed so much brighter whenever he was around.

"I've got to get my mind off of this wedding or I am going to hurl," Rachel announced, breaking Kinsley out of her thoughts. "Hand me my cell. I want to check my social media."

Kinsley reached over and grabbed her cousin's cell phone on the bench, handing it to her. "What? Are you going to go into withdrawal in Jamaica?" Jamaica was their honeymoon destination and Jamison had already told Rachel that the cell phones would not go with them.

"Shut up," Rachel said with a grin as she thumbed through her phone, her smile dying as she stared at her phone.

"What? Did someone die?" Kinsley asked. "Don't cry for god's sake. You will ruin your makeup."

Rachel looked up and Kinsley felt the first stirrings of dread in her stomach as she saw the look on her cousin's face. "Damn Kinsley, I'm so sorry," she said softly, handing over the phone. Kinsley took it and looked at the picture, her heart dropping into her stomach. The image looked as if it was taken across the street, the zoom distorting the characters slightly but there was no doubt on who it was. Jarred was standing on the sidewalk, his arms at his side as Susan was pressed up against him, her lips on his. The caption said something about them getting back together but to Kinsley it didn't matter. All she saw was that kiss. Jarred was kissing Susan.

"Aw honey," Rachel said, her skirts rustling together as she walked over and hugged her. "I'm so sorry. This sucks."

Kinsley felt the tears start to form in her eyes and handed the phone back to Rachel, hugging her arms around her waist to combat the overwhelming pain that was forming in her chest. Jarred had cheated, on her. After everything they had done, how she had stood up for him to her boss. The sex, oh god he'd cheated on her! She couldn't take this. With a sob, she turned away, looking out of the window. Why now?

"Kinsley," Rachel said, laying a hand on her shoulder and giving it a squeeze. "I, I really don't know what to say. I know you loved him."

"I love him," Kinsley whispered. That wasn't going to disappear because of one picture or after a week or a month or even a year. She had fallen head over heels in love with a man that she thought she could trust, a man that she thought had really opened up to her. But she had been wrong and the crushing pain was the result.

A knock sounded on the door and Kinsley swiped at her tears before turning to face Rachel with a wobbly smile. "Come on, let's get you married."

Rachel looked at her, concern in her eyes. "Kinsley, I don't think—"

"No," Kinsley interrupted. "I'm not going to let this destroy this day." She would fall apart later. This day was about Rachel and Jamison. Her life could wait.

Kinsley

THE CEREMONY WENT off without a hitch. Kinsley pasted a smile on her face as she watched Rachel tie the knot, inside falling apart bit by bit. Her life was in shambles now, her heart broken. She couldn't even stand to be in his presence but was going to have to be until she could tell him to bugger off and start rebuilding her life, without him.

After a dozen pictures, she walked into the reception hall with her escort, doing the little choreographed dance that the entire wedding party had worked on before falling into the crowd, dropping her posy on the wedding cake table as planned. An arm snaked around her waist, pulling her against a familiar body. Instead of the butterflies she used to have, now Kinsley only felt sick. "Hey beautiful," Jarred said against her ear, his hand caressing her stomach lightly. "What did I do to find you in a place like this?"

Kinsley bit her lip as she turned toward him, forcing her tears to retreat. She didn't want to cry in front of him or at this reception and ruin Rachel's special day. But she couldn't be in his presence right now.

"What's wrong?" he asked instantly, apparently seeing the emotions on her face.

Kinsley swallowed hard and stepped out of his reach, hugging herself. "You need to leave Jarred. You're not welcome here."

"What the fuck Kinsley?" he asked again, reaching for her. There was a small amount of panic in his eyes, coupled with hurt that she hadn't expected to see. It didn't matter. He had no idea how much she was hurting at this moment.

"No," she said, stepping away. "Get out Jarred."

His jaw clenched tightly. "I don't know what the hell has gotten into you. Talk to me, let me make it right."

She shook her head. "You can't make this right Jarred. We're over." Without waiting for a response, she walked away, retreating into the women's restroom before the tears started to fall. This was like a nightmare, a horrible nightmare that she wouldn't wake up from for a long, long time.

21

JARRED

Jarred leaned over the bed with a groan, wishing to hell that the ringing would stop in his head. Well, he wished that all of the whiskey he'd consumed would kill him straight off, but apparently he'd lived to see another bloody day. The ringing started again and he threw off the covers with a growl, his head pounding as he stumbled to the door, throwing it open. "What the hell do you want?" he said with a snarl.

"Good morning to you as well," his father said, his face darkening with anger. "What the bloody hell did you do to my assistant?"

"Bugger off," Jarred growled, attempting to shut the door. His father stuck his foot in the crack and pushed it back open, forcing Jarred to stumble back into the foyer. "Hell no. This is my flat and you will not kick me out of the place that I bloody well own."

"Fine," Jarred said, making his way back to the bedroom to gather his clothes. "I'll get the hell out." That was what everyone was telling him to do anyway.

He heard his father sigh loudly as Jarred started to pick up his clothes, throwing them on angrily. He didn't want to deal with his father right now. He couldn't. He could barely function as it was. "Jarred, stop."

Jarred turned around. "What the hell do you want me to do? What do you want from me?"

"I want you to tell me the truth," his father responded, his arms crossed over his chest. "You were never engaged to Kinsley to begin with were you?"

The sound of her name tore through Jarred's chest like a lightning bolt, causing the pain in his heart to increase tenfold. He missed her. Nothing felt the same since she had told him that it was over without an explanation, ignoring his calls and refusing to come to her door when he'd tried last night. It was like she had cut him out of her life just like that and Jarred never thought it could hurt so much. "No," he bit out, figuring it didn't matter. Hell he didn't want the money any fucking way. He wanted Kinsley.

"I knew it," his father said with a sigh. "Damnit Jarred, what did you do to her? She turned in her notice this morning."

"I don't know," Jarred said dejectedly, falling onto the bed, his head in his hands. "She just told me that it was over." He had replayed every waking moment before and after those words, trying to pick out the singular event that would be his downfall and nothing came to mind.

"I think I know."

Jarred looked up to see his father holding out his phone, a picture of a couple kissing on the sidewalk on the screen. It was then that he remembered. Bloody hell, someone had captured Susan's kiss the day of the wedding. "That's not what it looks like," he said immediately.

"Well, it sure as hell isn't a handshake," his father responded, pocketing the phone. "You love her don't you?"

"Who, Susan?" Jarred asked with a bitter laugh. "Hell no."

"No, Kinsley," his father corrected, a concerned look on his face. "You're in love with Kinsley."

Jarred idly rubbed his chest where the pain was, wishing that he could make it all go away. "Yeah, I love her." He wasn't ever going to love anyone the way he loved her.

His father sat down on the bed next to him, lacing his fingers together. "Son, I know we haven't had the best of relationships—"

Jarred let out a harsh laugh. That was an understatement. "You fucking hate me."

"I don't hate you," his father said softly. "I love you. You are my own flesh and blood."

"You think I'm a loser," Jarred reminded him, looking at his father.

His father shook his head. "I don't think that Jarred. I admit, I've always wanted you to apply yourself, live up to the potential that I know you have inside. My methods might have not been the best, but they were with the best of intentions."

Jarred sighed and rubbed a hand over his weary face. While he appreciated his father coming clean about the way he felt, it still didn't fix the fact that Kinsley was no longer in his life. She was gone and if she had seen that picture, was thinking the worst of him. Bloody hell.

His father stood and straightened his coat, a slight smile on his face as he walked to the doorway. "And my son would not give up on the woman he loves. A Maloney never gives up." He then turned at the doorway. "And tell my future daughter-in-law that she can have her job back if she chooses. She's one of my best employees and I would hate to lose her."

Jarred waited until he heard the front door close before a grin split his lips. Well his father was right about one thing. He wasn't a quitter by any means.

After a quick shave and shower, Jarred drove like a maniac to Kinsley's flat, a determined look on his face. She was going to hear him out, she was going to listen to his reasoning, the way that he felt about her. He would bloody crawl to Scotland if she wanted him to. But he was going to win her back. He had to.

Parking his car, Jarred jogged up the stairs to her flat, too impatient with the lift and reached her door, only to find it wide open. "Kinsley?" he called out as he walked through the doorway. "Are you here?"

A man in a striped suit appeared in the hallway, confusion on his face. "Are you my two o' clock appointment?"

"What?" Jarred asked, seeing that Kinsley's things were still in the flat. "Who the hell are you?"

"Hey buddy," the man said, holding up his hands. "I'm just the realtor. If you aren't interested in this place, I suggest you leave."

"She's selling?" Jarred asked, surprise filling his veins. Kinsley loved this flat.

"Yeah, just came on the market as of this morning," the realtor replied, a curious look on his face. "Why, are you interested?"

Jarred ran a hand through his hair, feeling dejected. She wasn't here and she was selling the only link he had to her. "Do you know where the owner moved to?" he asked. He had to find her.

The realtor shrugged. "Hell man I don't know. Maybe you can try the landlord. I'm sure he's got a forwarding."

Jarred nodded and turned to walk out the door, stopping before he reached it and turned around. "How much?"

22

KINSLEY

"Kinsley, darling, do you want to join us for dinner?"

Kinsley looked up from the book she was attempting to read, seeing her aunt in the doorway of the bedroom. "No, I'm just going to find something here."

Her aunt tsked, giving her a smile. "Darling you really should get out and about. It's been over a week and you haven't left not once."

Kinsley shook her head, hoping that she didn't look as dejected as she felt. "I'm fine. I promise I'll go out tomorrow."

Her aunt nodded and disappeared from the doorway, leaving Kinsley to the relative silence of her childhood room she used to share with Rachel. But Rachel was on her honeymoon and Kinsley was nowhere in her life: no job, no home, and no Jarred. The thought of his name caused her eyes to water yet again and she dashed them away as she heard the front door open and close, her aunt chattering to her uncle as they left for dinner. At some point, she was going to have to forget Jarred and move on, find another career that didn't run the risk of falling in love with someone like him. But her heart wouldn't let her move on. Her heart was still stuck on the man who had broken it and left it in pieces.

Kinsley sighed and threw the book on the bed, standing to stretch her aching muscles. Without the funds, she couldn't afford her flat anymore, not that she would have taken any funds to begin with. She would rather live out her life in a hovel than to accept any money for that ridiculous agreement. It had been doomed from the beginning and now she was forced to pick up the pieces.

The doorbell rang and Kinsley walked out of the bedroom to the front door, hoping it wasn't the kids next door again, selling those chocolate bars. She had already bought nearly a dozen. Opening the door, her smile faded as she looked at her visitor. Even seeing him made her chest hurt unbearably. "What are you doing here?"

Jarred's face didn't break out into a smile, his expression somber and cautious. "Hey beautiful."

"You, I have nothing to say to you," she stated, attempting to shut the door. He pushed back and opened it once more, his jaw clenched tightly.

"I, at least should be allowed to tell you my side of that picture Kinsley."

Kinsley crossed her arms over her chest, gritting her teeth. "Nothing you say will change the fact that you were kissing her Jarred."

He swore under his breath, running a hand through his hair. "Can I come in?"

"No," she stated, not wanting him in this house. She didn't even want him on the doorstep.

"Fine," he said, looking up at her. There was exhaustion on his face, some of the cockiness she was used to seeing no longer there. Instead, he looked, well, how she felt: hurt, torn, sad. "I did not kiss Susan. She kissed me. She had this sob story about how Baron was treating her and do you know what I told her?"

"What?" Kinsley asked. Jarred gave her a little smile then, though it didn't reach his eyes. "I told her not to settle."

"And she kissed you for that?" Kinsley said.

Jarred shrugged, sadness in his eyes. "I didn't kiss her. I would not fucking do that to you Kinsley. You are the only one I want to be kissing."

Kinsley tried not to let his words go to heart, but they were. He looked extremely upset, which thawed some of the anger she had built up around her heart, not wanting to get hurt again.

He stepped forward, his arms at his side. "I can't make up for the hurt Kinsley, but I'll tell you, I love you. I love you more than anything on this fucking planet. I literally can't breathe now unless you are in my presence. You occupy my thoughts. I want to see you in my bed every morning and kiss you goodnight every evening. I want to marry you, have kids with you. I've hurt you but I'll never hurt you again."

Kinsley's eyes welled up with tears as Jarred's words flowed over her, hearing what was coming from his heart. Did she dare to trust him? "I know it'll take some time," he continued, reaching into his pocket. "But I want to spend a lifetime making it up to you."

He reached for her hand and pressed a box in it. "You can hold onto that until you are ready. I'll give you the space you want but I won't give up. I'll never give up."

A sob escaped her and she ran into his arms, Jarred crushing her against him tightly. "I'm so fucking sorry," he breathed into her hair.

"It's okay," she forced out, clinging to him. "I love you, too."

He let out a shaky breath, kissing her neck lightly. "God, I thought I would never hear those words." Jarred pulled back and framed her face with his hands, his eyes searching hers. "I promise you, you will always be happy with me."

"I know," she answered, some of the tension and stress melting away. She believed him. Releasing him, she held up the box. "What's in this?"

"Our future," he said as she cracked open the lid. Inside, nestled in velvet, was a key. "I have a ring," Jarred added hastily, reaching into his other pocket and producing a gorgeous diamond. "But I thought you would want the key first."

Kinsley pulled out the key, turning it over in the palm of her hand. "What's so special about it?" she asked, looking up at him.

He grinned. "It's the key to your flat. I purchased it for us."

He had bought her flat, one of the things that had meant so much to her. If that wasn't an expression of love, she didn't know what was. With a cry, she threw her arms around him, placing kisses all over his face. "I love you," she said in between the kisses.

"And I love you," he laughed. She hugged him close, her heart overflowing with love for Jarred. It was going to be okay, they were going to be okay. He was where her heart lived.

"Hey," he said, kissing her neck once more. "Do you want the ring?"

"Later," she said. They had other things to do first.

EPILOGUE
KINSLEY

Eight Months Later

"You look beautiful Kinsley. It's so funny to be on this side of the fence this time."

Kinsley looked at the dress in the mirror and grinned, knowing exactly what Rachel meant. It was hard to believe that just a few months ago she had been a bridesmaid and now she was a bride, about to walk down the aisle to the man who had made her so unbelievably happy over the last few months. She woke up every morning thinking that today she was going to finally hit the peak of her love for Jarred and every night she realized that it was never going to happen. Every day she fell in love with him just a little bit more.

With a sigh, she turned around, looking at Rachel's bump that was barely visible under the material of her dress. "Well, I did not have that going on last time."

Rachel touched her stomach protectively, a soft smile on her face. "Yeah well things happen on your honeymoon. Don't forget that."

"I won't," Kinsley laughed, thinking of the wonderful honeymoon that she and Jarred were going to embark on after the reception. She couldn't wait. It had been a present from her soon to be father-in-law, a chance to tour Europe at their leisure. While the father and son relationship was still a work in progress, Kinsley felt that they had made huge strides in mending their decades' long feud. With the Formula One season bound to start in another month, she was going to enjoy this time with her husband. Jarred had really taken to the racing team, working on becoming an integral part of the team itself and expanding his role to a more hands-on approach. They had already joked about how she wasn't going to see him much once they kicked off and he'd assured her that he couldn't sleep without her. The argument had been quickly solved.

A knock on the door caused Kinsley to shake out of her thoughts, giving Rachel a brave smile. "Are you ready?" Rachel asked.

Kinsley nodded, her heart hammering in her chest. "I've been ready." She was about to marry the love of her life, the man that she was destined for. She couldn't get there fast enough.

THANK you for reading MR. TROUBLE! I hope you enjoyed BOOK 1 in the London Billionaires series.

Join me back in London for a swoony older brother's best friend romance? Zach promised he'd show Emma around London. Keep her out of trouble and that sort of thing. Only problem is Emm Welsh is the one woman he's always wanted. The one he could never have.

Order Mr. Big now so you don't miss it!

And you can read Alec and Jaya's story right now! Find out what happens when a desperate with a capital D event planner needs a date to her sister's wedding…to her ex-fiance. USA Today Bestseller!
One-click Sexy in Stilettos now!

> *"Sexy In Stilettos by Nana Malone is a fast-paced contemporary romance. Ms. Malone has delivered a book that is well-written. The characters are amazing, making this book fun to read. Jaya is fired from the family business by her ex-fiance that will soon become her brother-in-law. Alec's been summoned to help the*

family when his brother disappears. Alec and Jaya's story is like a whirlwind in a book, there's plenty of drama, humor and smokin' hot sex along with a little action and suspense."
— *Bookbub Reviewer*

Can't get enough billionaires? Meet a cocky, billionaire prince that goes undercover in Cheeky Royal! He's a prince with a secret to protect. The last distraction he can afford is his gorgeous as sin new neighbor.

His secrets could get them killed, but still, he can't stay away...

Read Cheeky Royal now!

Turn the page for an excerpt from Cheeky Royal...

SNEAK PEAK OF CHEEKY ROYAL

"You make a really good model. I'm sure dozens of artists have volunteered to paint you before."
He shook his head. "Not that I can recall. Why? Are you offering?"

I grinned. "I usually do nudes." Why did I say that? It wasn't true. Because you're hoping he'll volunteer as tribute.

He shrugged then reached behind his back and pulled his shirt up, tugged it free, and tossed it aside. "How is this for nude?"

Fuck. Me. I stared for a moment, mouth open and looking like an idiot. Then, well, I snapped a picture. Okay fine, I snapped several. "Uh, that's a start."

He ran a hand through his hair and tussled it, so I snapped several of that. These were romance-cover gold. Getting into it, he started posing for me, making silly faces. I got closer to him, snapping more close-ups of his face. That incredible face.

Then suddenly he went deadly serious again, the intensity in his eyes going harder somehow, sharper. Like a razor. "You look nervous. I thought you said you were used to nudes."

I swallowed around the lump in my throat. "Yeah, at school whenever we had a model, they were always nude. I got used to it."

He narrowed his gaze. "Are you sure about that?"
Shit. He could tell. "Yeah, I am. It's just a human form. Male. Female. No big deal."

His lopsided grin flashed, and my stomach flipped. Stupid traitorous body...and damn him for being so damn good looking. I tried to keep the lens centered on his face, but I had to get several of his abs, for you know...research.
But when his hand rubbed over his stomach and then slid to the button on his jeans, I gasped, "What are you doing?"
"Well, you said you were used doing nudes. Will that make you more comfortable as a photographer?"

I swallowed again, unable to answer, wanting to know what he was doing, how far he would go. And how far would I go?

The button popped, and I swallowed the sawdust in my mouth. I snapped a picture of his hands.

Well yeah, and his abs. So sue me. He popped another button, giving me a hint of the forbidden thing I couldn't have. I kept snapping away. We were locked in this odd, intimate game of chicken. I swung the lens up to capture his face. His gaze was slightly hooded. His lips parted…turned on. I stepped back a step to capture all of him. His jeans loose, his feet bare. Sitting on the stool, leaning back slightly and giving me the sex face, because that's what it was—God's honest truth—the sex face. And I was a total goner.

"You're not taking pictures, Len." His voice was barely above a whisper.

"Oh, sorry." I snapped several in succession. Full body shots, face shots, torso shots. There were several torso shots. I wanted to fully capture what was happening.
He unbuttoned another button, taunting me, tantalizing me. Then he reached into his jeans, and my gaze snapped to meet his. I wanted to say something. Intervene in some way…help maybe…ask him what he was doing. But I couldn't. We were locked in a game that I couldn't break free from. Now I wanted more. I wanted to know just how far he would go.

Would he go nude? Or would he stay in this half-undressed state, teasing me, tempting me to do the thing that I shouldn't do?

I snapped more photos, but this time I was close. I was looking down on him with the camera, angling so I could see

his perfectly sculpted abs as they flexed. His hand was inside his jeans. From the bulge, I knew he was touching himself. And then I snapped my gaze up to his face.
Sebastian licked his lip, and I captured the moment that tongue met flesh.

Heat flooded my body, and I pressed my thighs together to abate the ache. At that point, I was just snapping photos, completely in the zone, wanting to see what he might do next.

"Len…"
"Sebastian." My voice was so breathy I could barely get it past my lips.
"Do you want to come closer?"
"I--I think maybe I'm close enough?"
His teeth grazed his bottom lip. "Are you sure about that? I have another question for you."

I snapped several more images, ranging from face shots to shoulders, to torso. Yeah, I also went back to the hand-around-his-dick thing because…wow. "Yeah? Go ahead."
"Why didn't you tell me about your boyfriend 'til now?"
Oh shit. "I—I'm not sure. I didn't think it mattered. It sort of feels like we're supposed to be friends." Lies all lies.
He stood, his big body crowding me. "Yeah, friends…"
I swallowed hard. I couldn't bloody think with him so close. His scent assaulted me, sandalwood and something that was pure Sebastian wrapped around me, making me weak. Making me tingle as I inhaled his scent. Heat throbbed

between my thighs, even as my knees went weak. "Sebastian, wh—what are you doing?"
"

Proving to you that we're not friends. Will you let me?"
He was asking my permission. I knew what I wanted to say. I understood what was at stake. But then he raised his hand and traced his knuckles over my cheek, and a whimper escaped.

His voice went softer, so low when he spoke, his words were more like a rumble than anything intelligible. "Is that you telling me to stop?"

Seriously, there were supposed to be words. There were. But somehow I couldn't manage them, so like an idiot I shook my head.

His hand slid into my curls as he gently angled my head. When he leaned down, his lips a whisper from mine, he whispered, "This is all I've been thinking about."
Read Cheeky Royal now!

NANA MALONE READING LIST

Looking for a few Good Books? Look no Further

FREE

Sexy in Stilettos
Game Set Match
Shameless
Before Sin
Cheeky Royal

Royals
Royals Undercover

Cheeky Royal
Cheeky King

Royals Undone
Royal Bastard

Bastard Prince

Royals United
Royal Tease
Teasing the Princess

Royal Elite

The Heiress Duet
Protecting the Heiress
Tempting the Heiress

The Prince Duet
Return of the Prince
To Love a Prince

The Bodyguard Duet
Billionaire to the Bodyguard
The Billionaire's Secret

London Royals

London Royal Duet
London Royal
London Soul

Playboy Royal Duet
Royal Playboy
Playboy's Heart

The Donovans Series
Come Home Again (Nate & Delilah)
Love Reality (Ryan & Mia)
Race For Love (Derek & Kisima)
Love in Plain Sight (Dylan and Serafina)
Eye of the Beholder – (Logan & Jezzie)
Love Struck (Zephyr & Malia)

London Billionaires Standalones
Mr. Trouble (Jarred & Kinsley)
Mr. Big (Zach & Emma)
Mr. Dirty (Nathan & Sophie)

The Shameless World

Shameless
Shameless
Shameful
Unashamed

Force
Enforce

Deep
Deeper

Before Sin
Sin
Sinful

Brazen

Still Brazen

The Player
Bryce

Dax

Echo

Fox

Ransom

Gage

The In Stilettos Series
Sexy in Stilettos (Alec & Jaya)

Sultry in Stilettos (Beckett & Ricca)

Sassy in Stilettos (Caleb & Micha)

Strollers & Stilettos (Alec & Jaya & Alexa)

Seductive in Stilettos (Shane & Tristia)

Stunning in Stilettos (Bryan & Kyra)

~ ~ ~

In Stilettos Spin off
Tempting in Stilettos (Serena & Tyson)

Teasing in Stilettos (Cara & Tate)

Tantalizing in Stilettos (Jaggar & Griffin)

Love Match Series
*Game Set Match (Jason & Izzy)

Mismatch (Eli & Jessica)

Don't want to miss a single release? Click here!

Printed in Great Britain
by Amazon